# BACKGROUND FOR MURDER

In a psychiatric hospital, the head doctor lies dead — his skull smashed in with a brass poker. Private investigator Jacob Chaos is called in by Scotland Yard to investigate. But there are many people who might have wished harm upon Dr. Royd: the patients who resented his cruel treatment methods; the doctors who harboured jealousy of his position; even his own wife. With Dr. Helen Crawford as the Watson to his Holmes, Chaos must untangle the threads of the mystery . . .

*Books by Shelley Smith*
*in the Linford Mystery Library:*

THE LORD HAVE MERCY
COME AND BE KILLED
THIS IS THE HOUSE
THE CELLAR AT No.5

SHELLEY SMITH

# BACKGROUND FOR MURDER

*Complete and Unabridged*

**LINFORD**
*Leicester*

First published in Great Britain

First Linford Edition
published 2017

A catalogue record for this book is available
from the British Library.

ISBN 978–1–4448–3492–5

Published by
F. A. Thorpe (Publishing)
Anstey, Leicestershire

Set by Words & Graphics Ltd.
Anstey, Leicestershire
Printed and bound in Great Britain by
T. J. International Ltd., Padstow, Cornwall

This book is printed on acid-free paper

# 1

## 'Plenty of People Who Might Have Done It'

My first glimpse of the place appalled me. The nightmare of some insane Victorian architect. Turrets, battlements, minarets and gables affronted the skyline, and the sooted, red-brick face was pocked with innumerable small, deep-set windows.

I drew up outside the door and switched off the engine. A scowling little man in a wasp-striped jacket jumped out at me.

'Didn't you see the notice? Visitors are not allowed to park here at this time of day.'

I pocketed the ignition key and stepped out. 'I have an appointment with Dr. McIvor,' I said.

Without speaking he ushered me into the hall, pointed me to an upright wooden seat, and disappeared round the corner.

I sat there and waited. I had a hunch that it was going to be a messy and tiresome case, and I wished I hadn't agreed to take it on.

I don't officially work for the Yard, and a private investigator gets pretty used to picking and choosing his cases. But you can't very well refuse a job for the Yard. They had asked me to handle it because they wanted it to be done quietly, hushing up any possibility of scandal. Murder in a hospital can raise a pretty big stink. If it was taken over by the Yard — and, obviously, it could not be dealt with locally — the public would be bound to hear of it, and there would be all sorts of publicity; but, if managed by someone whose connection with the Yard had never been made official, then they stood a chance of hushing it up. So here I was. And I didn't like it.

The sour-faced little man bobbed up at me. 'Come this way, please.'

Along a dim corridor and up some unexpected stairs. The geography of the place was as confusing as the outside. The porter tapped on a door and opened it for me.

It was a pleasantly furnished rectangular room. At the far end, his back to the window, a man sat at a desk, waiting. The door closed behind me.

'Dr. McIvor?' I said.

He sat there and watched me coming across. Professional instinct, I suppose, but it didn't make me think much of his manners. I held out my card.

I said briefly, 'I am Chaos.'

'Please sit down,' he said smoothly. I sat in the chair facing the light from the open casement windows. His face was in shadow, his hands occupied in straightening the blotter on his desk.

'This is a bad business, Inspector,' he began.

' '*Mr.*', please,' I interrupted. 'So much simpler.'

'Well, Mr. Chaos.' he amended, 'I feel decidedly awkward about all this. How much do you know already?'

'It will be easier if we assume that I know nothing. Then you can start and tell me all about it from the beginning.'

'I'll do my best.' He smiled. 'It was on Monday morning, three days ago, that Dr. Maurice Royd was murdered. He was the Head of the hospital; and I, as the doctor with the longest record here, am temporarily in charge.

'Dr. Royd had presided at our customary morning meeting, at which the usual medical and general problems were discussed. This meeting generally lasted from about eight-thirty to nine-thirty. Afterwards, we all dispersed to our separate consulting-rooms as usual. Dr. Royd was not, so far as we know, seen alive again. His body was discovered by a patient over an hour and a half later. He was seated at his desk, and his skull had been battered in from behind by a poker that habitually hung to one side of the grate. He had been struck with the heavily ornamented base of the poker. At the moment it is in the hands of the local police being tested for finger-prints or something, but I suppose you can get it from them later. What else do you want to know?'

'You aren't telling this very well, you know.' I smiled.

4

He rubbed his forehead. 'I'm not used to this sort of thing. The shock and the confusion have made me rather ... uncertain. There has been lots to see to, and we have been trying to keep it quiet — even from the patients, but that is going to be impossible.' He turned to the window as he spoke, and I saw that the skin was bruised a dark grey under his eyes, and there were lines of strain about his narrow mouth.

'I appreciate that you are going through a very difficult time,' I said. 'But the more you are able to help me, the more I can help you.'

'I rely on you, Mr. Chaos. At all costs, any talk or scandal must be avoided ... the good name of the hospital ... it means so much to me ... ' His hands shook ever so slightly.

'I shall do everything in my power, Dr. McIvor,' I assured him smoothly, 'and now let us get back to the routine at hand ... I shall want to see Dr. Royd's consulting-room; I would like to know who the other doctors are; and, finally, I need a list of Dr. Royd's patients.'

'You can see Dr. Royd's room whenever you wish, and I will get you out a list of his patients — those he was recently attending. As for the other members of the staff, you will meet them all for lunch in the Common Room. Beside Dr. Royd, there are five of us: Dr. Chumly, Dr. Ennis, Dr. Fortescue, Dr. Crawford, and myself.'

'But you have been here longest?'

'Yes. Eleven years' seniority over any of the others. I have been here seventeen years, if I remember rightly. So you can understand to what extent I have the welfare of the place at heart.'

'I see. Of course, you realise that I shall have to talk to all the other doctors, and also to the nursing staff and the patients. Now, what — '

'Is it absolutely necessary for you to interview the patients? I did want it kept from them as much as possible. They are so easily disturbed by anything of this kind; it might even set back their treatment by months.'

I shrugged. 'You must understand how I am placed, sir. One of your

6

colleagues has been murdered, and — presuming that it was not worked from outside — somebody on these premises was involved. It is unavoidable for me to question them. But I do agree that it should be made as easy as possible. The medical and nursing staff, of course, present no difficulties; but the patients ... How would you suggest I tackle them? Would you mind if I strolled around for a while and got my bearings? It might be feasible to mingle with the patients for a bit, and see if it is practicable to pass myself off as one of them.'

'Yes, try it,' he suggested. 'It might produce the desired results. In any case — ' He rose to his feet. ' — I am in your hands.'

'A moment, Dr. McIvor,' I said. 'Have you any idea yourself as to who might have had reason to commit this crime?'

He looked astonished. 'No; none at all.'

'Did Dr. Royd have any enemies?'

'Not that I know of.'

I said, casually, 'What sort of a man was he? Was he popular with his colleagues? Did his patients like him? Did *you* like him?'

He looked embarrassed. 'I should say that, on the whole, his patients either loved or detested him. That is not unusual in this profession, but in his case it was even more pronounced — mainly, I think, on account of his stringent methods of analysis. As for the staff, well — he was their chief. There may have been petty grievances, of course, but generally speaking I should say he was definitely admired and respected.'

'And your personal feelings toward him?'

He hesitated. Somewhere a gong reverberated. 'Ah, lunch,' he said brightly. 'Come along, Mr. Chaos, and meet the rest of us. They will probably be able to help you more than I can. And we will doubtless be able to arrange our time and work so that we can be of more use to you. I myself have not only my patients and some of Dr. Royd's to handle, but also all the administrative side as well. A place like this entails a lot of work, Mr. Chaos. Indeed, I am a little tired; there is so much to see to . . . ' He chattered on. It was obvious that he was merely talking in order to steer me round an awkward corner.

He conducted me down the stairs to the end of the corridor and ushered me into a small dining-room, conventionally furnished with oak and leather chairs.

Dr. McIvor said, 'This is Mr. Chaos, who has come to . . . ' He paused awkwardly.

A fresh-faced man in his late twenties offered me his chair shyly. 'Won't you sit down? My name is Chumly, by the way.'

McIvor reasserted himself. 'Dr. Fortescue, may I introduce you to Mr. Chaos.'

For some reason, it had not occurred to me that any of the doctors would be women. Dr. Fortescue was a quiet, elderly, tweed-clad woman. She shook my hand and smiled vaguely.

'And Dr. Ennis.' The rotund little man who had been staring out of the window bounced towards me, held out his hand, and shook mine vigorously.

'How do you do. This is going to be very interesting. Always wanted to meet a chappie from Scotland Yard. Very interesting to see how their methods compare with ours. Though, perhaps, not quite the happiest circumstances.'

'I'm not from the Yard, you know.'

'But they asked you to handle this, didn't they? Comes to the same thing,' he assured me cheerfully.

The parlour-maid came in with a tray and, after a little confusion, we seated ourselves round the table. There was one vacant place.

Dr. Fortescue said, 'You know, we'll have to get rid of the Wylie child, she's being a nuisance.'

'I told you she wasn't suitable; she's obviously being over-stimulated. That's the trouble with all these hysterics,' said Dr. McIvor, dabbing mustard on his potato.

Cries of, 'Shop, shop,' from Chumly.

The door opened and the men half-rose from their seats. A woman of about thirty-five came in: tall, slender, with the facial dignity and beauty of Queen Alexandra, the resemblance heightened by the sleek chestnut row of curls along her forehead. I guessed that this was Dr. Crawford, and thought fatuously, *last but not least*.

She sat down in the vacant chair beside me, and said to the company in general, 'I'm sorry I am late. No.36 sent out an S.O.S. for me just as the gong went.' And then, 'Won't somebody introduce me to the gentleman on my right?'

'Let me introduce myself,' I said quickly, 'I am Jacob Chaos. And you must be Dr. Crawford.'

'And I deduce that you are our sleuth. Am I right?'

'My dear Watson,' I said admiringly. And somehow the atmosphere was lightened.

'Chaos,' she murmured reflectively. 'What a very inappropriate name for a detective.'

'Not really. Its deceptiveness is all part of my technique.'

'I see. Well, I suppose you've been shown over the place, and so on. Have you found any digs yet, or has one of us offered to put you up?'

Ignoring her first two questions, I told

her that I should probably be putting up at the pub I had passed in the village.

Dr. Ennis had said it was quite a sound place and they would do me pretty well. He was sorry he could not put me up himself, but his family was already overflowing out of the windows.

'Do none of you sleep on the premises?'

McIvor shook his head. 'We have rotation night-duty up till midnight, and after that, if there is a night-call, Dr. Chumly takes it. He lives just outside the lodge gates.'

'The Junior gets all the dirty work.' Chumly sighed dolefully.

When we reached the cheese stage, I said, 'Look here, I shall need to get some kind of a report from you all as soon as possible. Right now, I am going to have a look at Dr. Royd's room, and after that — ' I looked about me. ' — I would like to see you, Dr. Fortescue.'

'Certainly. I doubt I shall be of much use to you, though. I was on holiday when the — er — tragedy took place. I returned directly I was notified, of course, but I only arrived yesterday.'

'Well, in that case,' I said, 'we might postpone our interview to some later date.'

She looked relieved, and I wondered whether it was merely because she could get on with her work in peace. She seemed the typical spinster who lives for her job.

I decided then to interview Chumly first, then Ennis, and lastly Dr. Crawford. Luncheon was over; we rose to our feet. Dr. McIvor conducted me in nervous silence to his deceased colleague's room.

It was an attractive, though rather sombre, room. To the right of the door was a couch, tweed-upholstered, and beside it an easy chair. A bookcase ran along the length of the left wall. Some apparatus stood between the end of the couch and the beginning of the fireplace, on the other side of which there was a deep, worn leather chair set well back in the shadow. Under the wide window was a plain knee-hole mahogany desk, its swivel chair placed with its back to the glass.

I said, 'You saw the body before it was

removed, I presume.'

McIvor nodded. 'Yes, he was sitting there. The chair slightly pulled out . . . with its back inclined toward the fireplace. He was writing . . . he wouldn't have seen anyone coming up behind him.' McIvor gulped.

I raised my eyebrows. 'He must have heard them. Moreover, he must have known whoever it was was in the room, since he could see the door from where he was sitting.'

McIvor nodded. 'I suppose so.'

'What was he writing?'

'He was making up the notes on one of his cases. He was always keen on keeping his files up-to-date.'

'Hmm! I shall want to see those notes later. Unless, of course, they have already been handed over to the local police authorities.'

He seemed surprised. 'Dear me, no. They didn't even ask about them. It touches on professional secrecy, too. I shouldn't think they'd be of much use to a layman, though; most of those sort of notes are rather cryptic.'

'I'll be glad to have them all the same,' I said firmly. 'Now then, will you tell me in more detail just what you know occurred on the Monday morning?'

'According to his lists, Dr. Royd had an appointment from half-past nine to ten with a male patient, a Mr. Gresly. But he never turned up for his interview, we have since discovered. His next patient was a Miss Brace, scheduled from ten to ten-forty-five. Miss Brace waited in the passage outside during that time, expecting Dr. Royd to come out of his room to fetch her as usual. At about ten to eleven, Mr. Martin, the next patient, appeared. Miss Brace and Mr. Martin then hung about for a further ten minutes, and eventually Mr. Martin decided to knock on the door and walk in. It was he who discovered the body. It was Miss Brace's screams that brought Sister Hythe on the scene. She dealt very capably with both Miss Brace and Mr. Martin, and sent for me immediately.

'I didn't need to examine the body to see that life was extinct. To the best of my knowledge I touched nothing. I locked the door and phoned for the police. When they came — '

'That's all right,' I said, 'I can get all that from them in the official report. What did you do till they came?'

'I attended to Miss Brace and Mr. Martin, who were both suffering from shock in varying degrees; sent a sister round to cancel the rest of Dr. Royd's appointments; and . . . oh, I remember that I informed the rest of the staff.'

'Yes. And what were you doing yourself from nine-thirty till Sister Hythe sent for you at eleven?'

'Seeing patients. I'll give you the list and you can verify it quite easily,' he said curtly.

I thanked him, and asked him to send me Dr. Chumly as soon as possible.

Chumly came in and announced with nervous boldness that he considered he had a perfect alibi, as the Monday in question had been his free day. He explained that they used a five-day week, with one free day and rotation Sunday duty.

How did he spend his free day? I wanted to know.

'Oh, I stayed in bed and read most of the morning. Got up about noon, and caught a train to town, where I attended a medical convention. Spent the evening with a friend and returned by the last train. I didn't hear a thing about all this business until the next day.'

'You have a maid or a relation in the house?' I queried.

'I have a daily woman who comes in for a couple of hours in the morning to tidy up the place and get me my breakfast and so on. I'm not in much, you see,' he explained apologetically, 'and I have all my other meals over here.'

'And what time did your daily woman leave on this Monday?'

'About nine or ten, I suppose,' he said vaguely.

'So that during the actual hours when the murder was committed, you were alone, and I have only your word for it that you were actually in bed in your cottage?'

He went pink with indignation. 'Good heavens, man! Are you by any chance suggesting — '

'I am merely pointing out to you that

your — er — alibi is not quite so watertight as you assumed. However, let us leave that for the moment. How long have you been here?'

'Just on eight months.'

I plied him with harmless questions until he simmered down. The impressions I gathered from our subsequent conversation were that he found his work absorbing; that he quite liked, but was not intimate with, any of his colleagues — on account of his youth and newness to the place; that he could think of no reason why his chief should have been murdered: he didn't *know* of any enemies; that he had thought Dr. Royd a very great man, and his death a great loss to the psychiatric world and humanity. I sighed, and sent him away with a message for Dr. Ennis. I prowled about the room, waiting for him. Behind the deep leather armchair lay a folded screen. I pulled it away. A door was set flush in the wall. And it was locked.

There was a knock, and I turned to greet Ennis.

'Ah, Dr. Ennis! I wonder if you could tell me where that door leads to.'

'It leads to the squash courts. The courts used to be the doctors' common-room in the old days, hence the connecting door. But I don't think it's ever used now.'

'I see. Is the key usually kept in the door?'

'I've no idea. I suppose so.'

'Well, never mind. Let's return to Monday's murder. Would you describe your movements from nine-thirty to eleven a.m.?'

'I left the meeting at nine. From nine to ten I saw four patients. At ten I drove a patient of mine into Garrangarth to see a surgeon. We arrived back at about a quarter to twelve. The matron informed me of the disaster immediately, and I went straight to Dr. McIvor to see what I could do.'

'That's all very neat and circumstantial,' I said, cheerfully. 'But why did you go to Dr. McIvor rather than any of the other doctors?'

'As he is the most senior officer here, it seemed obvious to me that he would be in charge — at least, temporarily. It has happened before. I mean, when the Committee, for instance, have been deciding on a new medical officer or something of the sort, Dr. McIvor has always taken office for the time being. He ought to be Head himself, poor fellow! He's just had no luck at all. It's a pity, because he's a very good chap in his own line, and very keen on administration too. I think he feels his position pretty badly, you know.' He shrugged. 'Sorry, I'm digressing.'

I stared at him sharply, but his chubby face was bland.

'Did Dr. McIvor and Dr. Royd get on well with one another?'

'Oh, Lord! I expect he quarrelled with him occasionally; we all did. It was almost our customary routine for getting awkward questions settled. But Dr. McIvor is a quiet sort of man; he doesn't go in for rows. Unlike Dr. Crawford, who raises the roof when she can't get her own way.' He chuckled.

'And how did you get on with Dr. Royd? What did you think about him?'

Ennis pursed his lips. 'Not bad,' he

20

said. And then: 'To tell you the truth, I think he was the wrong person for the job. He wasn't interested in the administrative side; he was an analyst first and foremost.'

'And out of professional hours?' I asked. 'As a man?'

'I never found him particularly interesting, but then I've never been exactly enthralled by any of my colleagues. I should say he was quite a nice chap.'

'It's odd,' I mused, 'how you all tend to avoid that question.'

He said, slowly, 'I suppose no psychologist really cares to judge another human being.'

'However,' I continued, tartly, 'to the best of your knowledge he had no enemies, and you can think of no reason why he should have been murdered.'

'Quite the contrary,' he remarked, calmly, and walked to the door. 'There are plenty of reasons why he should have been killed, and plenty of people who might have done it. But that's your pigeon, my dear sir.'

I let him go, and wondered what had

brought about the sudden change of manner in him; what had so quickly turned his smile into a sneer.

Dr. Crawford came through the open door, her eyebrows raised, 'What have you been doing to Dr. Ennis? Giving him the third degree? I met him outside looking very unhappy.'

I edged away from it noncommittally and started the usual routine. She had been interviewing patients during the fatal hours, and had been told by the matron at Dr. McIvor's request just before the police arrived on the scene. Again, I asked what manner of man he was.

'I don't think we ever quite hit it off together.' she admitted. 'Our methods of treatment were so diametrically opposed. So you can appreciate that I would rather not say too much about him. I may be biased.'

'Apart from his work, what manner of man was he?'

'I should think his wife could answer that better than I.' She smiled.

I was irritated that no one had so much

as mentioned the fact that Royd was married. It necessitated a complete reorientation of my scheme.

I said, 'Do you know what has happened to the key of the connecting door there?'

She frowned. 'No, I can't even be sure that there is one.'

'You never saw Dr. Royd, or anyone else, use that door? Not even in the days when it lead to the common-room?'

'Oh, then, yes. I wasn't thinking . . . ' She was perceptibly flustered.

'Perhaps I should have made myself clearer,' I soothed. 'It isn't important, anyway.'

'But it is important! It provides another exit or entry for the murderer . . . if one can *prove* that it has been used recently.'

'Watson, thou shouldst be living at this hour!' I exclaimed genially. 'That is really very bright of you. Now, I wonder if you can solve another little problem for me. One of your colleagues suggested to me that there were plenty of reasons and plenty of people to assassinate Dr. Royd. What do you suppose he meant by that?'

23

'I cannot possibly answer for the opinions of someone else,' she said icily.

'Oh, my dear Watson.' I sighed. 'All right, if you won't help me, you won't.' I dismissed her, made up my notes, and decided before I went any further to report to the local station.

# 2

## 'All This Free-Love is Wrong;
## it Ain't Moral'

Inspector Trevor was a delightful, unpretentious little man, who greeted me with open arms and seemed glad that an unpleasant case had been taken from him and handed over to an outsider.

'Sit down, Mr. Chaos. I've got the reports here all ready for you.'

'Thank you. What do you think about it all?'

'I think it smells'

I agreed with him. 'What about Royd's wife? And did he have a family?'

'He didn't have any children, if that's what you mean, but then he's not been married long. As for Mrs. Royd, she's a nice little thing and good to rest the eyes on. But I shouldn't be surprised if he bullied her.'

'Have you got a photo of him? I'm

getting the most confused impression of this man. If you have, put it in with the reports, will you. Oh, and I'd like to have a look at the 'blunt instrument', if you don't mind.'

'Yes, it's just come back from the experts. They report no fingerprints except some blurred ones — undoubtedly Royd's own. Fragments of skin and hair and so forth on the base, also Royd's. Here it is.'

He handed me the poker and I scrutinised its heavy weighted base. I balanced it on my outstretched palm; it had the size, shape and poise of a shillelagh.

'A perfect weapon,' I commented, 'just the sort of thing one might snatch at unintentionally in a blind rage, or build up a carefully premeditated crime about.'

'Not premeditated,' Trevor asserted. 'I'd wager that one of his patients just got in a temper, picked it up and copped him one.'

'Why?'

'What else would you expect a loony to do?' he said angrily.

'I thought the whole point was that they were not loonies.'

'Oh, they're not supposed to be, I know, but some of 'em are as near the bughouse as you could wish.'

'So you think it was a nut who didn't know what he was doing. Any particular one in your mind?'

'No. It might have been almost any of them. I don't envy you the job of sorting out their alibis! I know that trying to find a murderer among the nuts would have made me ripe for a bughouse myself.'

'Maybe it wasn't a patient.' I sighed hopefully. 'It seems that quite a lot of the staff haven't got anything in the way of alibis. But alibis don't mean a thing, as you very well know. It's the *motive* that's going to get me down. McIvor has a motive *and* he has an alibi; Chumly has no alibi but likes him; Ennis dislikes him and has an alibi, and the same goes for Dr. Crawford; Dr. Fortescue is out of it, and thank God we can dismiss somebody. I haven't even looked at the nursing staff or the domestic staff or the patients, or anyone from outside. Huh! It looks as if you're going to see a lot of me, my friend. And if you want to know who I think did it, I'll tell you: Mrs. Royd.'

'You're crazy,' he gasped. 'Why her?'

I picked up the case portfolio and smiled sourly, 'Just so that I can ignore the loony-bin and all its inmates. Good night to you, sir, you'll see me again all too soon.'

I found my way to The Three Crows, booked a room, and ordered my dinner to be sent up. I had that dossier to study. I put the car away, unpacked my bags, and rang for a bottle of whisky and a siphon. When it came I poured out two fingers, kicked off my shoes, and lay down on the bed with the dossier beside me.

I took out the five photographs of Dr. Royd. Four taken of the deceased from different angles . . . and a nasty mess he looked. The fifth was a studio portrait. It showed him seated at his desk, his right hand holding a pen, his left flat on the paper, and he glanced upwards as if surprised in the act of writing a prescription. He must have been hand-some: a well-built fellow, with a straight nose, a black curly beard, large enigmatic dark eyes, and a noble dome-like forehead — the good effect of which was counteracted by the small mean mouth with its cruel narrow lips.

I measured myself another whisky and began looking through the statements made to the police at the time of the murder. On top of the list were the statements of Royd's patients. Gresly stated that he had not felt like having an interview so he had gone for a walk. When asked where, he replied, 'Nowhere in particular.' He didn't know how long he had been out; he didn't know what time he had returned; he never paid any attention to the clock. He announced gratuitously that he loathed Dr. Royd, but when pressed for a reason he remained silent.

Miss Brace had been unable to give a statement. She was prostrated by shock. Mr. Martin, too, appeared to be some-what shattered, judging by his incoherent remarks, the gist of which was to the effect that he had never thought to see anything like that, and that he couldn't think how it had happened.

Then there were some brief statements from various patients confirming the alibis of Dr. McIvor, Dr. Crawford and Dr. Ennis. Nothing very interesting there.

The landlord interrupted me in order to serve me an excellent dinner. The studio portrait, lying face upward on the bed, caught his eye.

'Ah! That's the poor gentleman who was done in, isn't it?' he remarked, with relish. 'Ah, well! We all get our just deserts,' he said, piously.

'Just deserts?' I queried.

He nodded. 'They say the goings-on up there are something awful. I always will say that all this free-love is wrong; it ain't moral.'

'What free-love business are you talking about?' I frowned.

'I'm telling you: this Frood they all think so much of up there encourages the doctors to go in for all this free-love with the poor loonies.' He paused, impressively.

I was shocked. '*What are you talking about?*'

'You ask anyone: they'll tell you the same. Folks say that the loonies come out of them rooms, their hair standing on end and their clothes all anyhow — just as if they been in a rough-house.' He thought for a minute with wrinkled brow. ' 'Free association'; that's their name for it,' he added triumphantly.

I received the news solemnly, and got him out of the room as soon as I could. When he had gone, I lay down on the bed and gave way to my suppressed laughter. I finished my meal, ran through the rest of the dossier, and went downstairs for a breath of air before beginning to write my own notes on the case.

It was darker now, and a heavy ground-mist was rising. The air was pleasantly fresh, fragrant with night-stocks. I breathed it in deeply and leant back against the hedge.

A small car pulled up beside me with a jerk. Dr. Crawford pushed her head through the window. 'Hullo!' she said. 'I was hoping I'd run into you.'

'You nearly did,' I remarked, feebly.

She laughed politely. 'I — er — wanted

31

to apologise. I behaved badly this afternoon, and I'm sorry. Your job must be quite hard enough without people making things more difficult . . . I'd much rather help you than hinder you,' she concluded, shyly.

'Well, that's very nice of you,' I said. 'How about having a drink on it?' I opened the car door for her as I spoke.

The bar-parlour was empty. I ordered a gin and tonic for Dr. Crawford and whisky for myself. While I waited for the drinks, I watched her reflection in the mirror behind the bar counter. She leant against the overmantel, slender and taut in a bluish-grey tweed suit the colour of her eyes. She was too attractive to be a doctor, I thought, absurdly, and wondered just why she had chosen that admirable profession. At this point the barmaid slid the drinks across the counter towards me. I picked them up and returned to the table.

'Why is it,' I wanted to know, 'that locally the hospital is regarded as an asylum?'

She smiled. 'The ordinary person has

no conception of the meaning of 'nerves'; to them it is merely a polite way of stigmatising lunacy. After all, people do behave very queerly when their nerves are disordered to any extent.'

'Queerly enough to account for them committing murder?' I asked.

'Yes, definitely. That brings us back to the end of our conversation this afternoon; that's what I wanted to talk to you about. I may be able to help you. Of course, you were quite right: there are too many people who might have done it; people who had a reason for doing it. I — we all felt how very much better it would be for all concerned if it could be proved that the crime had been committed by someone with no connection to the hospital. I realise now, though, that a crime cannot be solved like that. So I say, yes, it is a definite possibility that some patient struck down Dr. Royd.' She took off her horn-rimmed glasses and polished them absently on the soft lining of her driving-glove.

She looked a different person without them, her expression at once softer and sweeter. I wondered if that was why she wore them. I said, 'It really is very nice of you to give me your confidence. It will make my work immeasurably easier if there is someone to help me deal with these technical, psychological points.'

She nodded and settled the glasses over her face again. 'There are 'technical' points, as you would say, that you cannot hope to know of. Do you understand me if I say that I could more easily accept the situation if Dr. Royd had been struck from the front instead of from behind?'

I confessed myself at a loss.

'You see, it is unlikely that Dr. Royd would allow a patient to get behind him. You can never be sure that a patient will not suddenly attack you at any moment. And, therefore, we all take the precaution of always keeping the patient within our range of vision. Some of them would never dream of attacking their doctor, being much too scared of the consequences; others will throw something or themselves at you if you so much as blink an eyelash.'

'That does make a difference,' I admitted.

'I only said it was unlikely. I may be wrong. It may have been a patient Dr. Royd felt he could trust, or he may have forgotten to guard himself for just that necessary instant.'

'Thank you,' I said, 'you have been very helpful. We won't talk about it any more now, you look tired. Perhaps ... ' I hesitated. 'If I have difficulty with the patients, might I ask you to help?'

'Of course.' She stared at me searchingly. 'Look here, I am due for a week's holiday the day after tomorrow. I don't suppose I shall be allowed to leave the district during the investigations, shall I? So what if I took that week off just the same, and then I could be at your disposal, free to give you whatever help lies in my power?' She stopped expectantly.

'That would be wonderful,' I said enthusiastically.

'I should have to get Dr. McIvor's permission,' she mused, 'No reason why he should object, though. He must be as anxious as any of us to get this ghastly thing cleared up.'

'Do you realise all you are taking on?'

'I'm not afraid of danger.' She smiled.

'Oh, I didn't mean that you would be in any danger. I meant that it is possible that I should not need you much at all, that your week off might be wasted. How would you feel about that, Doctor?'

'I'll take the risk. I'll talk to Dr. McIvor about it tomorrow.' She stood up and collected her gloves and bag. 'I must go now; it's late. Good night, Mr. Holmes.' She held out her hand and grasped mine firmly.

'Good night, Dr. Watson.'

# 3

## 'You Mean, You Think I Killed Him'

When I stepped into the hall next morning, the sullen porter glanced up from his ledger and gave me a sulky 'Good morning.' A plump woman in a tight maroon uniform hurried down the stairs. She stopped and eyed me questioningly.

'I am Matron. Can I help you?'

I thanked her, gave her my name, and told her that I wanted to look around.

She nodded. Dr. McIvor had spoken of me to her, telling her I was to have free run of the place and any assistance I needed — so if there was anything she could do . . . ?

I asked her where the patients would be found at this time of day.

'Most of them are not up yet,' she said, 'but they'll be downstairs soon. Occupations start in half an hour; and, except for a few cases who have been exempted by their doctor, attendance is compulsory from nine-thirty to twelve-thirty. It's one of the few rules we have. It keeps them from brooding too much, makes them concentrate and gives them the feeling that they are still useful,' she rattled off proudly. 'Now, while we are waiting, would you like to be shown around? I don't suppose you've seen the place properly yet, have you?'

I suffered myself to be led away.

'Now, down there are the servants' quarters and all the domestic side; kept quite separate from the rest of the building, you see. Of course things *are* rather disorganised at the moment because of this wretched business . . . This is the dining-room . . . I have never been so horrified in my life, I assure you. How *anyone* could have done such a *wicked* thing, I don't know . . . And these are the public rooms: the library and reading-room, the main drawing-room, the gentlemen's lounge and smoking-room, and a little rest-room . . . Such a *terrible* shock it must have been for his poor little wife ... That's the main staircase ... And I *have* heard that the poor soul is — ' She stopped abruptly. 'I mustn't gossip like this. Whatever will you think of me?'

I made polite noises of dissent, but she wouldn't talk any more. She showed me in quick succession the billiard-room, the dance-room, and the squash-court that held a ping-pong table in the middle. All these rooms, I noticed, had connecting doors which were heavily soundproofed.

'I won't take you upstairs, because there is nothing to see but the bedrooms, really. Unless, of course, you're particularly interested. I would like to show you the grounds, though; we grow all our own produce, you know. And we have a tiny model farm for poultry and pigs. Oh, dear! How time does fly, to be sure. It's much too late to take you round the grounds now; occupations have already started.' And she hurried me out of doors towards a large wooden building of super-functional modern style, its southern side composed entirely of glass.

'Isn't it lovely?' said Matron enthusiastically. 'We use it for our dramatic productions, too. Not all of them work indoors, I must tell you; it depends on the state of their health. A lot of them are outdoors, on the farm — grooming the horses, keeping the grass-courts in condition, gardening, and so on. However, you'll find enough to start with in here.

'Tell me,' she continued, 'do you want to be introduced or anything? Or are you incognito? If so, I'll tell the Occupation Officer about you, and she'll leave you to go your own sweet way. Would that be better?'

I nodded gratefully. The woman had plenty of common sense.

I slipped over the threshold, and quietly absorbed the scene. Thirty or forty people of both sexes were engaged in every imaginable variety of innocuous occupation. Spinning, weaving, sewing, knitting, basketry, pottery, clay modelling, leatherwork, pewter-work, carpentry and toy-making were in progress all over the place. There was noise, talk and laughter; people strolled up and down, or stood about in little groups. Nobody paid the slightest attention to me.

I edged over to the nearest group and sat down unobtrusively on a nearby stool. A large woman, precariously balanced on her backward-tilted chair, whittled away at a small block of wood. Opposite her a thin, morose-looking youth was knitting a long strip of a charming Fair Isle design.

'So what are you going to do?' she was saying. 'Ennis can't take any more; he's overworked as it is; and I don't suppose McIvor would take you. Besides, you don't like him either, do you?'

'I'll carry on like this till the new bloke turns up, I suppose. If he's any good, I'll stay; if he's not . . . I'll have to leave. I've a good mind to leave, anyhow. There's no point in my staying; they can't do anything for me. I'm hopeless.' A large tear slid gently down the side of his nose. 'Maurice was the only one who really understood me; and now that he's gone, Molly, I tell you, the outlook is pretty bloody.'

'You ran him down enough while he was alive, didn't you?'

'Oh, shut up!' His voice quavered. 'We all do it, don't we? It doesn't mean a thing. Fundamentally, whether they're beastly or not, we have to rely upon them absolutely. It's cruel of you to throw in my face all the things I've said about him in the past.' More tears fell on the woollen strip.

'Don't take on so. I didn't mean it, Denis. Now, dry those pretty eyes and pull yourself together.' There was an undercurrent of contemptuous cynicism in the loudly soothing voice.

He said: 'You're a hard bitch, Molly,' and walked away to the far end of the room, his coloured balls of wool trailing along the floor behind him.

The woman called Molly turned to me, eyebrows raised. 'Poor Denis; he does get so worked up over trifles. You been here long?' she demanded, with a swift change of subject.

'Just arrived,' I said, truthfully.

'I shouldn't think you'd be here long,' she informed me, reassuringly. 'But you mustn't let a little scene like the one you've just witnessed upset you. You'll get used to that sort of thing after a while. You'll probably find yourself behaving like that, too.' She laughed.

'I hope not. What are you making?'

'It's meant to be an ashtray for my dear doctor. A farewell present. I'm leaving shortly, thank God! And I expect my beloved Dr. Crawford will be glad to be rid of me at the price of an ashtray,' she said, coarsely.

'What's Dr. Crawford like?'

'Are you under her?' she asked.

'I'm not sure, I may be.'

'She's not bad, as they go. Tough, you know, but rather a pet. If you get on the right side of her, you're all right; but heaven help you if you don't hit it off.'

'Let's hope we do, then. Tell me about some of the patients. I feel rather lost here.'

'I know. The first few days are hell in a place like this . . . Well, what would you like me to tell you about the patients? You know it's one of the strictest rules of the place that one is forbidden to discuss one's own or other people's ailments,' she warned me, and winked.

'I guessed that. What puzzles me, though, is that some of them seem to be perfectly well.'

She smiled at me pityingly. 'That doesn't mean a thing. Some people put up a good show; others don't fight at all. You look pretty well yourself.'

I pointed to a group leaning languidly against the opposite wall: three women and two men; their faces grey and drawn, their eyes swollen with recent tears. 'What's the matter with them? They look ill and unhappy, as if every ounce of fight has been knocked out of them.'

'It has,' she said, tersely.

'There are others who look just as bad,' I continued, 'but it's their crowding together speechlessly like that which looks so awful. The others sit apart in their misery; they cling to one another.'

'Bright boy!' she commended. 'The ones who sit apart are the ones whose misery is not caused by the outer world, but by their own feelings; they know no one can help them, and it is better to be alone. The others — who cling together, as you neatly put it — are suffering from the shock of an external situation common to them all; it is disaster through no fault of their own, and the knowledge that they are all suffering from the same blow makes them seek the solace of each other's company. Whew! Didn't I express that beautifully?'

I nodded comprehension. 'And the tragedy common to them all is Dr. Royd's untimely demise?'

'Good God! Have you heard that already? Well, I don't know who told you about it, but I wouldn't mind betting that most of it was a lot of guff. A lot of rumour gets around in a place like this. There has been a lot of hush-hush business about it, but that's only natural in the circumstances. They have to try and keep these things quiet for fear of upsetting the patients . . . besides giving the place a bad name. Why, they even hush it up when a patient kicks the bucket, and this is twenty times more important.

'No,' she continued, 'if you've heard that he did himself in or anything like that, you take it with a large pinch of salt.

I've heard it suggested that Brace and Martin — two of his patients — are being kept away from us because they know too much. They are supposed to have discovered him. But, even if they did, there is no reason to suppose it happened in what they call 'suspicious circumstances'. They're not the only ones to have been prostrated by this. It's vile to change doctors in the middle of treatment, anyway, let alone because he's died on you.' She paused, and then continued brightly, 'Well, let's change the subject. And I shouldn't mention it to any of the others, if I were you; at least half of them don't know that anything has happened.'

'I'll remember that. And now — '

'And now,' she interrupted me hastily, 'I must fly, or I shall be late for my appointment.' She brushed the shavings from her skirt, pocketed the knife and wooden block, flung the chair from her and rushed away.

From the corner of my eye I saw Denis sidling towards me. He sat on the edge of the table. 'Molly gone? I suppose she was telling you all about me.'

'We weren't talking about you. As a matter of fact, she was telling me about Dr. Royd,' I said.

'Oh, she was, was she? Scandal-mongering old cow! She ought to have more sense — '

'But I had already heard about it; you mustn't blame her. In fact, I don't think she knows much about it. After all, she wasn't a patient of his . . . that must make a difference.'

'It does,' he said, gloomily, and lapsed into silence.

'I'm awfully sorry for you. But, still, it wasn't your fault, was it?'

'Hell and damnation!' He clutched my arm tightly. 'The whole point is that it is my fault. I had an interview with him that morning and I never went to it. If I had — ' He spaced out his words slowly. ' — he might never have been killed.'

'Killed!' I echoed. 'Was he *killed*?'

'Yes!' He writhed. 'And I might have saved him. It might never have happened.'

'Why did you cut your interview?'

'I was furious with him. I hated him. God help me! I fought him all along the line. You'll know what it's like yourself soon; you just can't give in to it. And it wasn't only that. I hated him for knowing too much about me — knowing more than any other person alive — '

I said: 'You won't have to worry about that. He's dead, and his knowledge died with him.'

His eyes gleamed. 'What are you driving at?'

'You hated him. He knew too much. And now he's dead. How very convenient for you!' I was coolly insolent.

He shook violently. 'You mean, you think *I* killed him.'

'You said you went for a walk.'

He licked his lips. 'Yes. But — but if it couldn't be proven? They would think . . . You think — ' His mouth fell open. Then he drew himself up and sneered: 'Maybe I did kill him. So what?'

Molly whirled across and smote him on the shoulder. 'Hullo, tuppenn'orth! How's that for a lousy interview? Ten ruddy minutes, all told! She must be in a hurry to get rid of me.' She drew out the wooden ashtray as she spoke, and commenced chipping at it. 'Well, have you two been getting to know one another? Damn! I'd as soon not have an interview at all as one like that. I'm all on edge, curse it! What has happened in my absence? You do look ghastly, Denis. What's up?'

Denis said slowly, viciously, 'This charming gentleman has just accused me of murdering Dr. Royd.'

Molly's comment was 'Oh!' in a high, surprised voice. She looked down at her lap. My eyes followed hers, and I saw that her comment was unrelated to Denis's speech; the little knife had skidded on the wooden surface, and now neatly skewered the ball of her thumb. The blood was dripping freely on to her lap.

Denis, too, was staring at her hand, his eyes starting from his head, his face a horrid yellowish-green. I was just in time to catch him as he dropped . . .

# 4

## 'McIvor Disliked Him'

I had to get away. I couldn't stand that oppressive menacing atmosphere, those unpleasant tortured people. It nauseated me.

Dr. Crawford came briskly up the drive toward me. I pulled myself together and greeted her.

'Hullo! Aren't you staying to lunch?' she said.

'I'm lunching at The Three Crows,' I told her.

'Oh, don't do that. Something's upset you. You mustn't let the place affect you. It will only make your job harder if you do. Come back with me and get it off your chest.'

'I won't, if you don't mind. Look here, why don't you come down to the inn and lunch with me there? Then we can talk in peace,' I suggested.

She hesitated. 'They don't approve of that sort of thing here. But Dr. McIvor has given me permission to help you, so I presume it will be all right. Yes, I'll come.'

I fetched my car, and we drove down in silence to the inn. We had a couple of cocktails apiece and went into the dining-room. When the waiter had gone to execute our orders, she turned to me.

'Now then, what's the matter?'

'It goes against the grain to fight sick people,' I said. 'They have enough to contend with without my bullying them and trapping them into saying things they don't want to.'

She smiled thoughtfully. 'Don't pity them too much. They're as wily as the devil. They're always suspicious and wary of people — of normal people, that is. I don't think you'd ever get past them on your own; that is why I offered to help you. You'll need me.'

'I will,' I said, trying to assimilate her point of view. '*You* ought to know what you're talking about on that subject. It doesn't make me like it any better, though.'

'Then we'll leave it for the time being. Tell me what happened today.'

I repeated briefly the gist of my conversation with Molly and Gresly. When I had finished, she said: 'That seems perfectly obvious. What's worrying you about it?'

'It's anything but obvious. Let's take Molly first. She's your patient. Ready? How friendly is she with Gresly?'

'Hmm! I think she's quite fond of him, in a maternal sort of way. He confides in her.'

'Yes, I gathered that. But either he doesn't confide in her to the extent she imagines, or she did know that Royd was murdered and she hid it from me. I wonder why?'

'She may have believed you were a patient, and so for your sake and from loyalty to the hospital she would deny it.'

'All right. Why did the knife slip? Was she startled by what Gresly said? Did she stab herself deliberately? And, if so, why? Was it to distract our attention? Or an attempt to shield Denis? Or to show *me* his reaction?'

She was taken aback by my spate of questions.

'I can't answer you,' she said at last. 'But all our training — like yours, I expect — teaches us not to jump to conclusions. I want to turn it over in my mind, and I'll speak to Molly about it too.'

'I didn't expect an answer,' I reassured her. 'I only wanted you to haul me up if any of those categories were impossible, so we could rule them out.'

The waiter served us with fried point steak, mushrooms and *sauté* potatoes, and refilled our glasses with Beaune.

'Ready for some more questions as you eat? This time it's Gresly. We won't bother with how he knew Royd had been killed. But why did he tell me? We presume that he didn't tell Molly, so why confide in a stranger?'

'Don't we always prefer to confide in a stranger?'

'Yes, but not someone you are going to see again. And why did he lay himself open to attack like that? Was he merely being neurotic when he stressed the fact that he hated him so much? When he said he might have saved him if only he had gone to his appointment? Or does he *know* the exact time at which the murder occurred? And then, who is he shielding?'

'Oh, stop!' she implored. 'I thought you suspected Gresly of the crime. Now you seem to think he knows who did it and has some reason for shielding them. Who do you suspect?'

'But everyone!' I was surprised by her question. 'I'm trying to eliminate some of them, to make the thing simpler. No, Gresly is as much a suspect as anyone. What was he really doing when he said he was taking a walk? What was he doing in that period that he is frightened will be discovered? Well, all that's easy to discover; routine work, not psychological. But, again, why did he tell Molly that I had accused him of murder? Was it a warning? And why did he faint at the sight of the knife in Molly's hand? Does he always faint at the sight of blood? Or did it remind him of Royd's shattered skull?'

Dr. Crawford leant back in her chair

and closed her eyes.

'Sorry,' she said, faintly, 'it's just the recollection of that appalling sight. Even a doctor inured to death would have been shocked by it. Poor Maurice!' She was rapidly gaining a hold on herself, the colour flooding back to her face.

Awkwardly, we apologised to one another. She laughed, and the tension dissipated. 'Aren't we absurd?'

I accepted the cue she offered, and turned the conversation away from murder-detection and hospitals. It was all very nice and friendly. I watched her peeling a peach, and thought what nice hands she had. An immense topaz swung loosely between two knuckles on her left hand. I asked inanely what had made her train as a psychiatrist.

'A patient of mine once outlined three possibilities: 'It might be an intense love of humanity, an insatiable curiosity, or a desire to see and make people suffer.' It struck me as rather apt,' she said, smiling. 'I'll leave you to find which category fits me.'

I explained that I hadn't meant her, so

much as her colleagues in general. She shrugged.

'Look here,' I said, 'when you offered to help me, I thought you meant it in all sincerity. You've got to play ball with me. I want to know what the other doctors felt and said about each other. I want to know their backgrounds and their aims. And you're hiding your knowledge from me — '

'What a bully the man is!' she said, plaintively. 'Of course. I'll tell you anything I can. Ask away.'

And so, slowly, surely, I culled my information. What Dr. Crawford told me boiled down to this: Dr. Royd was very much a self-made man, of humble origin; he had struggled for his education, and fought for the money to study as a doctor. He had been chosen two years before by the board of directors (the Head in office having resigned owing to ill-health) on account of his brilliant qualifications as an analyst. And so he was of great benefit to about a dozen people — his patients — and a considerable liability to the rest of the hospital. Already on the down grade, the last five years of this due to administrative ill-management, Dr. Royd's incompetence in that direction made things chaotic.

It was understandable then that McIvor disliked him. To be supplanted by an inferior must have been exquisitely galling. No one knew why the Committee had so consistently overlooked him for the headship. However, his antagonism had never been open. He had continued working in his quiet efficient way, giving his loyalty first and foremost to the hospital. He had been happily married, but his wife had died. Since then, his interests were work and fishing. As a psycho-therapist he was not an advanced thinker; but, because of his extensive experience, was most effective with light cases and quick cures. And there lay another point of serious opposition with Royd, who dealt almost exclusively in severe cases, and was prepared to devote two, three, five years — or infinity — to them.

Dr. Ennis, on the other hand, was a robust little man, who enjoyed his work and was devoted to his family. Very much the extrovert himself, why he had chosen such an introspective profession was a mystery. All the same (according to Dr. Crawford), his extroversion had its advantages from the point of view of his patients, who adored him on the whole.

Mary Fortescue, who had the longest record after McIvor, was excellent with young women and specialised in hysterics. She was exactly the sort of woman she looked; and, like so many English spinsters, was passionately fond of her two dogs. She had spent her recent week's vacation with her married brother in the Lake District.

Chumly was still a 'new boy'. Any work he did now was likely to be of more value to his future patients than his present ones, who were merely providing him with the essential experience. He had only just got his degrees, and was really too young for the job, but Dr. Royd had needed someone cheap ... Hospital expenses were already too high. Dr. Crawford could tell me nothing more of interest about him. She said she had never paid much attention to him. Mainly, I gathered, because he was only too ready to cast sheep's eyes in her direction.

At this point, she suddenly became aware of the time and leapt to her feet. I thanked her, paid the bill, and drove her back to the hospital. That talk with her had done me good, and I had conquered my revulsion for the place. I felt comfortable and relaxed in her presence. I suppose that is part of a psychologist's training. I asked her if she would dine with me that night, but she refused on the grounds that she was on late duty.

As we negotiated the drive, I said: 'I've got to see the couple who found Royd as soon as possible. What doctor are they under now?'

'You won't be able to see Miss Brace; she's still seriously ill. I think she's under McIvor at the moment, but it's quite likely that Mary will take her over later. As for Martin, he is my patient now, so I suppose it's up to me. He isn't really well enough to talk about it, and I don't want to do the poor lad any harm.'

'Well, supposing you were present to give him confidence? You could advise me how best to couch my questions, too.'

She nodded slowly. 'All right. If I see that he is being seriously upset by it, I — we — you wouldn't mind my dealing with it? Postponing it, perhaps?'

I readily concurred. She thanked me absently for the luncheon. She was already submerged by the bright, rather severe, professional air she wore like a cloak on duty. We did not enter the hospital together.

# 5

## 'You Can't Kill a Man by Wishing Him Dead'

Dr. Crawford's consulting-room was gay with sunlight, and ran to pattern with a desk, two easy chairs, and a couch.

She said, 'I've sent a sister to fetch him. I think you had better sit in my armchair there — and I'll sit at the desk where I am less liable to distract his attention.' I nodded agreement and sat down to wait.

At length there was a tap on the door and a sister with a napkin on her head peered round the open edge. 'Mr. Martin, Doctor,' she said.

Martin was dressed in a silk dressing-gown over bright blue pyjama trousers, with leather slippers on his naked feet. He was unshaven. He seemed healthy enough — only the round blue eyes showing any sign of strain.

Dr. Crawford moved toward him. 'Mr.

Martin, this is Mr. Chaos. He wants to ask you a few questions. Will you do your best to answer him? Just sit down in your usual chair and take it easy.'

He sat down, his hands closed tightly round the arms of the chair.

I said, gently, 'Mr. Martin, I am trying to get to the bottom of Dr. Royd's death. I know all this must be as unpleasant to you as it is for all of us. So, let us try and get it over with quickly, shall we? Now, please tell me in your own words what occurred.'

'I've already made a statement to the police. I don't want to talk about it anymore!'

I swallowed hard. 'I appreciate that, and I wouldn't ask you to if it weren't absolutely necessary.' I was scribbling as I spoke. 'But, if it will make it easier, I'll ask you questions. Now then, how long were you waiting before you decided to go in to Dr. Royd?'

'I don't know, I was talking to Miss Brace. Ten minutes, quarter of an hour . . . '

'Yes. And what made you decide to go

in before the doctor came out himself?'

His fingers positively dug into the chair-arms. 'Well, Miss Brace had told me that she had been waiting for three-quarters of an hour . . . I thought — if he had been delayed with a patient upstairs or somewhere, he would have sent a message explaining or altering the appointment — So I — I went in to see what had happened.'

'What did you think had happened?'

'That he'd been taken ill — or something . . . ' he stammered.

'Did you think he might have been murdered?'

He jumped to his feet and shouted: 'I won't have it! I won't stay here to be tormented and insulted!'

I caught Dr. Crawford's eye and signalled appealingly. We'd never get anywhere at this rate . . . However, Dr. Crawford understood my signal, and was ready to take over. I slipped her my scribbled list of questions as I passed, relying on her to get answers by her method since mine was inadequate. From my seat at the desk I watched Martin as he stood there undecided. Nobody moved. Martin sat down again.

Dr. Crawford leant back and half-closed her eyes. 'Do you know why you got so excited just now when it was suggested that you had thought Dr. Royd might have been murdered — even before you went into his room?'

He made a conscious effort to relax. 'Don't you see, I don't know where I am or what it's all about . . . ? You don't know what these last few days have been like . . . And my head — my head!' He ran his fingers through his thick untidy hair.

'Are you frightened of being accused of the murder yourself?'

He breathed heavily; his eyes swivelled from side to side like frightened mice frantically pedalling the wheel in their cage. He didn't answer.

She said softly: 'How long were you alone in the room before you cried out and Miss Brace came in?'

His face was quite blank, and he remained motionless . . . At last, very slowly, he rose to his feet, and with a swaying movement made toward the door. His fumbling fingers got it open, then the outer door, and he stumbled from the room . . .

Dr. Crawford was on her feet and after him. When I heard them struggling in the corridor, I shot out after them. Then I saw Martin hanging half out of the landing window, held back only by the narrow iron bar that ran midway across it, and Dr. Crawford with her arms round his thighs.

I caught him under the armpits and hauled him in. He fell away from me, sat down on the floor, and began sobbing. Dr. Crawford leant against the window-bar to get her breath. She was as cool as ever. Mentally, I took off my hat to her: she was a fine woman.

She took Martin by the arm. 'Wouldn't you find it more comfortable in my room? You could lie on the couch and give way to your grief freely.' And Martin suffered himself to be led back again.

The sight of the man lying sprawled on the couch, crying helplessly, nauseated me. Was I supposed to drive sick men

— guilty or not — to suicide? I felt the need of a drink badly.

I murmured: 'I suppose you want me to go now. It would be cruel to bully him any more just now, but I'll *have* to see him later.'

'He'll be all right in a little while. Don't go yet. His resistance has broken down, you see. After this, he'll be glad to explain and get it off his chest.'

Gradually, his crying fit abated. Dr. Crawford poured him a glass of ice-water. He gulped it down and gave a hiccoughing sob, his awful exhaustion plainly visible.

'Feeling better? Then tell us all about it. There isn't any need to be so frightened, Mr. Martin. You can't kill a man by wishing him dead,' said Dr. Crawford, benignly.

'I'm sorry,' he said, meekly. 'I've made a fool of myself once again. I know that my wishes to kill Dr. Royd haven't anything to do with it. I mean, my intelligence tells me that that is not why he died. But what other people deduce — ' His gaze shifted to me and then back again. ' — is quite different. It isn't hard to find out in a place like this that one person hates another, and would like to kill him. We say these things here, but how much we mean them would be hard to prove.' His voice quavered. 'How could I prove that I had *not* murdered Dr. Royd? Who would believe me? It seems hopeless to me. The more one protests one's innocence — one's complete sanity — the more one is disbelieved.' He paused.

'I have publicly said on more than one occasion that I would like to kill Royd. I discovered the body, and was alone in the room for several minutes, before Miss Brace joined me. I think I was just standing, staring . . . Waiting for it to sink in. And when tackled on the subject, I tried to commit suicide. It looks as if I did it, doesn't it? It's the work of a lunatic, and I'm mad. Why should you believe me when I swear that I had nothing to do with it? Besides, that jumping out of the window looks bad; either I should have done it properly or not at all . . . Perhaps you even think I never really intended to kill myself — was just making a gesture, a double bluff . . . ' He gave a short bark of laughter.

I said, 'Thank you, Mr. Martin, for your frankness. I'm sorry it was so painful for you.' And then I added: 'Insofar as it is possible at a stage like this, when everyone is more or less suspect, I would like you to know that I don't think you have much to worry about now.' It was very unprofessional, but — poor devil!

His whole body slackened with relief, colour flooded his face. Weak laughter bubbled in his throat as he said, 'Oh, well, Mr. I've-forgotten-your-name — thank you so much for saying that.' Tears sprang to his eyes. 'If you don't mind, I'll go now, before I start getting silly.' The silk skirt of his gown fluttered round the edge of the door and he was gone.

'Thank God that's over,' I said, devoutly. 'I should never have got through it without your help. Poor chap! Of course, I should never have implied that he was no longer under suspicion. But he is cleared all right, provided nothing turns up to show that he could have murdered him earlier by some means. He certainly didn't do it when he discovered the body.'

She looked surprised, then said, 'I'm afraid I've got a lot of patients to see — '

'Of course, of course. I'll clear off now. See you later, perhaps.'

# 6

## 'You Seem to Take it for Granted that Fear Implies Guilt'

I wandered down to the hall, stuck my head inside the porter's cubby-hole, and said, 'What has become of the key to the connecting door in Dr. Royd's consulting room?'

'I don't know,' he barked irritably. 'You can't expect me to keep track of keys in an establishment like this. It isn't my job.'

I asked him whose business it was, then. He just shrugged.

'Well, which maid does the room? If you don't know,' I forestalled him, 'find out; and send her to me, please.'

He gave me a dirty look and ambled off in the direction of the servants' quarters. But the maid was similarly unhelpful. Yes, there was a key to the door. But she couldn't say how long it had been missing. The key had been there recently, she remembered knocking it out one day when she was polishing the doorknob. No, she wouldn't like to say when it was, not within a day or so.

Why the absence of the key worried me so, I'd no idea, but I had a hunch that if I could find it, it would tell me a lot. You could see how convenient it would be for the murderer to use that door. In the morning those three public rooms would almost certainly be empty . . . the murderer would be unobserved. Moreover, the crime could then have been committed any time between nine-thirty and eleven o'clock. On the other hand if that door had not been used, Royd must have been killed between nine-thirty and ten. Quite a difference. It would have been almost impossible, besides foolhardy in the extreme, to twice slip past Miss Brace unseen.

If the key had been removed or lost some time before his death, then his murderer must have used the main door. If I could only prove that, it would narrow things considerably. But if the key was removed after his death by the murderer, for one reason or another . . . well, then, I should have a job in front of me.

I dined alone at The Three Crows, and wished that Helen Crawford was sitting opposite me. So I ordered another dish of pie to sustain myself, and concentrated on a plan for the hours ahead of me.

I got back to the hospital just as the patients came out from dinner, headed for coffee in the large lounge. I followed them. It was a vast room with striped chintz covers on the overstuffed chairs and gaily covered cushions; heavy brocaded curtains covered most of the wall space, and there was an immense fire roaring at the far end of the room. There was a clatter of china coffee cups, a buzz and parrot-screeching of conversation.

A middle-aged woman with a weather-beaten complexion and a Midwestern accent, offered to pour me out a cup of coffee. She introduced herself as Miss Gellibrand.

'You're new, de-urr, aren't you?' she said. 'Well, I can tell you, you'll love it. Everybody's so kind here . . . Do you play bridge, or can't you concentrate?'

I shook my head ambiguously. 'What do they generally do here in the evenings?'

'We have an Amusement Board who are chosen from among the lot of us by popular vote. We have games and dances, musical evenings and competitions, and I don't know what all. We're supposed to be having paper games tonight, but the organiser has gone sick, so maybe it won't take place — ' She paused for breath, gulped down her coffee, and said, 'Come on over to the fire and meet some of the folk . . . They're just the nicest bunch . . . '

'The nicest bunch' were a mixed group: young typists with restless hands and giggles; depressed little bank clerks; Empire builders in the prime of life; and tough-looking blonde babes who, even if they'd given up drinking, were still smoking too much.

Under the surface was a dreadful despairing lifelessness . . . an appalling feeling of unreality. That idle chatter didn't mean a thing; the undisguisable anguish of their pleading eyes gave them away every time.

Across the room I could see Molly listening to Denis. Her hand was neatly bandaged and worn against her chest in a dark silk handkerchief tied slingwise.

Denis must have felt my gaze, for he stood up and said loudly, 'I feel like a game of pool, Molly. How about it? Let's go and see if the billiards room is free.'

*One to me*, I thought, as I watched them go. Even if Gresly couldn't stand to see me, he should have been more careful than to ask Molly to play billiards with him. You can't play with one hand.

I didn't want them around anyway. I addressed the man next to me: 'Doesn't the time drag awfully in a place like this?'

'In a way, yes. Sometimes the slowness of the individual minutes is enough to make you scream, and yet the end of the day comes with nothing to show for it. Weeks and months pass here with a sickening speed. Really.'

What luck! I'd rung the bell and got my penny back.

'I know what you mean.' I was serious, sympathetic. 'One day is so like another . . . with absolutely no distinguishing mark to tell them apart.'

He nodded. I tossed the ball to my Midwestern friend, saying, 'I know what these places are like. There may be plenty to do, but it's all so unimportant that it becomes meaningless. Can you remember what you did yesterday? Well, perhaps yesterday; but the day before that, or this time last week?'

The man at my side said firmly, 'You're quite right, sir.'

About half the people present showed an interest in the subject, either for or against.

I said, 'Supposing you had to remember what you did the night of today last week — how many of you would be able to, I wonder?'

Miss Gellibrand was heavily sarcastic. 'Well, de-urr, if I was in any doubt I'd simply look up the Amusement Programme for that day . . . I hope I'm not so far gone that I can't recall whether or not I participated in that evening's entertainment.'

'All right, you've won the first round. But let's try to find out which of us is right. There are about twenty of us here, aren't there? Fairly representative, no? Well then, let us see just how many of us can remember just where we were and what we were doing last . . . Monday — that's four days ago. Not the whole day, that would be too much of a good thing. How about the morning? From breakfast till luncheon last Monday. Agreed? Fine.' I was very much the Master of Ceremonies. I had to coerce them, otherwise they might have been too damned languid and bored to get going. 'Then I think we'll start the ball rolling with Miss Gellibrand. Come along, Miss Gellibrand, say your prayers and get your alibi ready.'

'Monday last . . . now let me see . . . I went down to the village,' she concluded on a note of triumph.

'Oh, no, that won't do. You've got to start from the beginning. What time did you wake up? Did you breakfast in bed? And so on.'

Slowly, by a mixture of persuasion, disbelief and jokes, I arrived at a pretty accurate description of the way she had spent her time that Monday. I couldn't go through all that paraphernalia with the rest of them — they'd too easily lose interest, and besides, there wasn't time.

'Look here,' I said, 'Miss Gellibrand has got through by the skin of her teeth, but it will take too long to do you all like that. It isn't fair, either, because hearing what other people say will help you to remember. So how about getting a slip of paper and a pencil and writing it down? If you give them back to me afterwards, I'll sort them through and publicly proclaim the winner.'

I saw them well settled down to it, said, 'No cheating, mind,' and strolled away.

I found Gresly alone in the billiards room, smoking.

He glanced at me, but said nothing. The lights over the table were not lit, and the cues were in their stands.

'Care for fifty up?' I suggested carelessly.

He nodded. While he collected the balls and switched on the lights, I inspected the cue stand. He came up behind me, and I remembered Dr. Crawford saying that they never let a patient get behind them. The air was quite still and I felt as if ants were crawling over my scalp.

His voice cut through the room abruptly. 'There are only two usable cues there . . . a sixteen-and-a-half, and a seventeen.' His hand shot over my shoulder and pulled one out. 'Try this.'

I glanced along its shining length. 'Thanks, this'll do.' I looked up and saw Denis smiling at me, secretively, maliciously. He knew he had frightened me, and knew that I now knew he had done it on purpose. Pretty!

A silver coin glinted in the air. 'Call!' he shouted. I called heads and it was tails.

Denis's first shot sent spot off red into the bottom pocket. I retrieved it and rolled it down the table to him. He repeated the action. The third time, I said, 'You'll have to give me twenty-five.'

His mouth quirked downward. 'It's finished now,' he said. 'I fluke like hell.' He left me red in baulk, and I couldn't do a thing. We had another half a dozen uninteresting shots, and then I made a break of seventeen.

He made another break of ten. I said, 'Now we're getting into it . . . Molly play a good game?'

He gritted out, 'Not with one hand.'

I said, 'I hope it doesn't pain her too much. I'm afraid it was your fault, wasn't it, Gresly? You startled her. Positively dangerous when you have a knife or some such weapon in your hand, or when the other person has.'

Gresly slammed hard and sent plain into the top pocket. 'Sorry,' he said gruffly. 'Need we have all this conversation while we're playing?'

'Why does it worry you so?' I said gently. 'Don't be so — ' I cannoned from spot to red, potted red and went in off. ' — so antagonistic.' I collected the balls and set them out.

'Antagonistic, my God! I would like to know by what right you come here and torment me,' he said bitterly. 'You're trying to frighten me, aren't you? But why?'

'If I am, I'm succeeding. You're terrified,' I said teasingly, and marked up 31-25 in my favour.

He stared at me angrily. 'I've got plenty to be scared about, believe me. But you seem to take it for granted that fear implies guilt; you think I'm hiding something from you . . . Oh yes. I know who you are, Mr. Chaos . . . I wish you were as clear as to my motives as I to yours.'

'I wish just that, too, Gresly.' And I was sincere.

He bent over the table and made a follow-through cannon. 'It's simple enough, isn't it? I'm in this infernal place because I'm ill . . . everything is upside down and distorted, I know it, and yet I can't see straight . . . And my whole life is bound by fear . . . a fear that passes over you in great waves, shaking at you until your soul is nearly shattered . . . '

I sighed. 'All right, Gresly, I'll take your word for it. Maybe I don't know what it's all about.'

I missed an easy cannon. The score stood at 40–47 in Denis's favour. He ran out on a break of five. I said, 'Thanks, Gresly. You won that game, but there'll be others all right.'

I could see by the set of his face that he thought me a hell of a sportsman. It was pretty mean at that. But he'd been handing me a sweet line for the last half an hour. Now it was up to him. I knew he wouldn't leave it there, and if I didn't make a move, he'd be certain to come to me himself eventually.

I left him and returned to the drawing-room to collect the alibis that were waiting for me — I hoped. When I returned to The Three Crows, I found Inspector Trevor off-duty, sitting in the saloon bar waiting for me. I bought two double whiskies and sat down beside him.

'Well,' he said, 'what's new?'

'You were right every time, Trevor: this job stinks.' I drained my glass. 'Listen to what I've found out today.' And I outlined the events for him,

He said cautiously, 'I don't think you want to take it too seriously that they all seem to have something to hide . . . that's the way they are.'

'It's too damn smooth,' I snapped. 'I'm certain that there was some honest-to-God reason behind all this, and that it was definitely premeditated.'

He raised his eyebrows. 'I sincerely hope you're wrong.'

'We'll see. Now, would you like to help me sort these alibis?'

Together, we checked them. Some had been in bed, some in the village or at Garrangarth, some occupating. Twelve had sound alibis reaffirmed by other people. Another seven were probably all right . . . this was just routine again. I reckoned that I had put the finger on half the patients in the hospital, and I sighed at the thought of those I still had to get some account from.

We were finishing our drinks as the barmaid carolled, 'Time, gentlemen; time, please,' and began switching off the lights.

Trevor said, 'I don't need much sleep. I shall be only too glad to honour you by accepting another little drink from you in the privacy of your room.'

I told him to help himself while I sprawled on the bed waiting for him to speak.

'Remember your first bet? Mrs. Royd

has not got an alibi worth talking about. According to her, she drove to the village and did some odd chores, and from there went up to the hospital to see her husband. She parked the car here, though, because — so she said — she wanted to walk. But she didn't see Royd. She said that when she got there she changed her mind, decided that it wasn't important, and could wait till the evening. So she walked back, picked up the car and drove home.'

He looked at me. 'It's *twenty minutes* from here to there. Forty minutes — say forty-five if you like — for both journeys. And the garage man says that she drove in as the clock struck ten — he happened to notice that; and she came back for the car as he was going off for his elevenses . . . between eleven and five past, as near as he can figure.'

I swore lengthily and expressively 'Are they doing it on purpose? My God! What a bunch! But we haven't yet got any proof that she went to the hospital at all.'

'What else would she be doing?'

I shrugged. 'Perhaps she had a

rendezvous with a boyfriend or something.'

Trevor said, 'Why should she then fake up a completely useless story about going to see her husband and then changing her mind? She's not that dumb. She's had time to think up something cuter than that.'

I agreed wearily. 'Did you manage to get from her what she wanted to see her husband about? If she is innocent and her story true, Royd might be alive now if she had seen him.'

'Oh, she said she wanted to ask him something about the guests she was to ask to a dinner party they had partially arranged for the weekend.' He pursed his lips disbelievingly. 'That's all I've been able to get for you so far. Sorry it hasn't been more helpful.'

'Maybe it's helpful, in the wrong way. Actually, the more tangled it gets now, the easier it should become, ultimately.'

'Oh, yeah?' said Inspector Trevor. 'Isn't that ducky?'

# 7

## 'I Lied to That Inspector Man'

Saturday morning was cloudless and sunny, suggestive of first frosts and bonfires, when all the countryside is an enchantment of subtle gradations of colour. I shaved at the open window admiringly, feeling exhilarated. I gazed up the hill to the distant clump of beeches that marked the hospital boundary on this side, from whence I thought I could hear the faint but rhythmic thudding of an axe on wood. It was all very peaceful and rustic.

While I wrapped a scarf round my neck, I ran over the day's routine in my mind. First, to see Mrs. Royd. She seemed to be a pathological liar; still, as the man's wife, she ought to know something. Would the widow be prostrated with shock?

After her, interview Royd's patients. I

ran my eye over the list. Miss Brace, Mr. Martin, Mr. Davies. Mrs. Harrison, Mr. Gresly, Miss Gellibrand — I hadn't noticed that Miss Gellibrand was one of his patients before — Mr. Green and Mr. Croft. Perhaps Dr. Crawford would help me with them; she had certainly been remarkably competent with Martin. A strange life for a woman, I thought, as I pulled on my jacket, ran through my pockets to see that all was in order, and departed.

The Royds' house lay apart from the village in the lowest fold of the valley. It was a small, over-restored cottage, which must once have been charming. The maid took my card and ushered me along a dim passage into an old-fashioned cottage garden. A small figure in black, with a trug full of dahlia heads, came towards me.

'Mrs. Royd?' I inclined my head.

'Yes. I'm afraid I don't know the name — ' I explained myself and my errand. 'Of course. Shall we sit down? There's a lovely view under this apple tree.'

I agreed that it was, and praised the garden while I examined her. She was exquisitely pretty; small, and all soft curves, golden curls, wide kitten-surprised blue eyes, a little snub nose with the faintest of freckles, and a curling rose-petal mouth. I reckoned she couldn't be more than twenty-four, poor kid.

' . . . it's very stubborn,' she was saying. 'It's so old that it just does as it likes. It doesn't matter how much I root a thing up, next year it pops up again as sturdy as ever.'

'I'm very sorry to trouble you at a time like this, but there are just a few points that I thought you might help me with. Had your husband been at all different lately? Was he preoccupied, irritable, or nervous?'

'No. He was just as usual,' she said calmly.

'Did he have any enemies that you know of?'

'Enemies?' she echoed incredulously. 'That sounds like a detective story!'

'Yes,' I said, soberly, 'only it's real. So your husband didn't confide any anxiety he might have felt to you?'

'Maurice wasn't the sort of person to confide in anybody.'

'I understand from Inspector Trevor that on the morning that your husband was killed, you were going to consult him about something or another, but changed your mind and went away without seeing him. Now, it appears this journey took over an hour instead of, as one would expect, forty minutes. Perhaps you stopped to talk to some friend, and had forgotten all about it when you were talking to the inspector, eh?'

She bent down and tugged at a weed in the path — the leaves tore from the stem under the pressure of her fingers. She sat up, a little flushed from her exertion.

'It was nice of you to give me a loophole. But I lied to that Inspector man. Not for myself; it was someone else's secret, don't you see. But I don't suppose it matters now. That morning, I didn't actually go to the hospital itself. I — I went to see Dr. Fortescue.'

'But Dr. Fortescue was away on holiday.' I frowned.

'Everyone *thought* she was away,' she corrected me. 'That was what she wanted them to think. Not my business to ask her why. But she asked me particularly not to tell anyone that she was back — so I didn't. Of course, I didn't really understand how important these seemingly little things are to you. I'm sorry if I've made extra work for you,' she said placidly.

'So you went to see Dr. Fortescue?' I said absently. 'In her own house, presumably? How did you know she'd be there?'

'She rang me up on the Sunday. I said I wanted to see her, and she suggested Monday about half-past ten.'

'Fancy that!' I said with absentminded levity.

'You aren't,' she burst out, 'for one minute trying to suggest that Dr. Fortescue had anything to do with Maurice's — death, are you?' She was pale and distressed now. 'Just because Dr. Fortescue does not wish everybody to know her private business, it is ludicrous to presume that she's a murderess. Why, if you knew her — '

'But, Mrs. Royd,' I laughed, '*I*'m not suggesting she's a murderess at all.'

She rubbed her forehead. 'I'm so sorry,' she said. 'I've not been quite myself lately. This — this trouble has rather upset me, I'm afraid . . . I'm very fond of Mary Fortescue — she's been like a mother to me.'

'It's only natural you should be upset . . . Is that Jersey Beauty, by the way? Quite my favourite dahlia. I'm not keen on size myself, and anything larger than that seems out of place to me.'

'Yes. I don't care for them much personally. I'm not a dahlia-grower, the soil is much too light here. Roses are really my specialty.'

'I can see that. Was Dr. Royd fond of gardening too?'

'Maurice's amusements weren't in that line at all.' She spoke almost absently.

'Well, I won't bother you any further. Thank you for explaining that little confusion to me. I can find my own way out quite easily. Goodbye for the present.'

I found the maid in the kitchen. I leant against the dresser. 'A light hand with 'pastry, I see,' I said approvingly.

'Coo-er! Oh, you made me jump!' One floury hand leapt to support her plump bosom.

'Guilty conscience, eh? Been double-crossing the milkman with the baker-boy — ?'

'Oh, go on with you. What d'you want?'

I'm frightfully good at that sort of thing. 'Domestic badinage' we call it in the profession.

She told me that she had not been there above five months herself. Dr. and Mrs. Royd had been married three or four years. They get on as well as most married folks, she reckoned. They didn't quarrel much. He mostly seemed to get his own way over things, she just seemed to give in to him. Particular? Lor, fussy wasn't the word for him. Everything had to be just so or he'd kick up ever such a dust. Funny bloke he was, for a doctor. He'd come out with some funny sayings; weird wasn't in it. No, she didn't suppose they were a very happy pair. Oh, well, she didn't pay any attention to gossip. No, the mistress hadn't seemed terribly upset when the news came through. She hadn't burst out crying, not got hysterical or anything; been more quiet and stunned like, poor little thing. Course, those loonies ought to be in straitjackets; they said some of them were ever so violent — this was proof of it, wasn't it? Ever so sad. Sad to be a loony, too.

I slipped out of the side-entrance and behind the beech hedge to the gate. Through the drawing-room window, I could see Mrs. Royd telephoning. I wondered if it was to Dr. Fortescue to warn her. Well, I should soon know.

Dr. Fortescue's cottage was the other side of the hospital grounds; about half an hour's walk from Royd's — which was down in the valley and the far side of the village — I reckoned. Perhaps less if I cut across country. I decided to risk it.

I strode briskly across a field of stubble. On my right, three sycamores stood against the horizon, the branches a black lace fan against the evanescent blue of the autumn sky. Everything was very quiet, and I could hear bird and animal cries, children playing, a distant drone of traffic, a nearby tractor, and the turbulent throb of an aeroplane. The scarlet leaf of a Turkish oak fluttered towards me . . .

I walked briskly up the steep hillside, traversed a little stream, and went through a copse to an old stone wall that bounded the hospital estate. I fumbled along it for a few hundred yards till I came to a half-hidden gate — padlocked, but low enough for me to scramble over. I was in the miniature beech-wood I had seen from my bedroom window.

A voice to the right of me shouted sharply and I leapt in the air. A tree hurtled through the air towards me and crashed with a vibrating thud just a few yards away.

A group of men came through the trees. One shouted, 'It nearly hit him! Did you see that, you chaps, it nearly hit him! My God, it nearly hit you, sir.'

A stalwart young man broke from the group and came towards me, his brown eyes anxious. 'I say, sir, are you all right? It didn't actually touch you, did it? It must have given you a scare, though.'

'It missed me. It's quite all right.'

A very wide man now joined us, panting heavily. He looked like a good-natured but flustered frog swelling visibly from mingled indignation and embarrassment.

'We're not entirely to blame, you know,' he panted, 'you shouldn't be round here at all. Are you — trespassing?'

I shook my head, smiling.

'A new patient, then? Funny, we didn't see you coming — oh, I see, you climbed over the gate. No, I don't think it's ever used now, except the way you used it — after hours, perhaps. Well, I'm glad the damage is no worse.' He nodded. 'Should have thought you'd have heard the axes, though. Weren't trying to commit suicide, were you?'

'About as much as you were trying to murder me.' I smiled. 'Is this your occupation, by the way?'

'Yes, good hefty work, keeps you in good condition,' said the stalwart young man.

'Damn sight too hefty for me,' panted the wide one, mopping his forehead. 'Thank God it's autumn. I shall ask to be transferred to leaf-sweeping.'

'Come on, you chaps,' shouted the man who seemed to like shouting, 'We'd better cut the branches off, hadn't we?'

I asked the wide man to direct me to Dr. Fortescue's cottage, picked my way across the outlying branches, and left them — immediately reabsorbed in their work.

The maid ushered me into a tiny sitting-room decorated in a soft blue and grey chintz. The ceiling was too low for me to stand comfortably, so I perched on the arm of an upholstered armchair. A black spaniel hurled itself at my knees. By the time he had completely rewashed my face, Dr. Fortescue came in.

'I'm glad you've made friends,' she said quietly. 'Do sit down and be comfortable.' She surveyed me kindly from huge grey eyes. She sat down, took the exuberant spaniel on her lap, and waited patiently for me to begin.

'I expect you know why I've come, Doctor. I've been to see Mrs. Royd this morning.'

'Dear child,' she murmured.

'She told me that she had been up to see you on the Monday morning, during at least part of the time in which we suppose Dr. Royd to have been murdered. Is that so?'

'Yes, she came to see me.'

'We understood that you were away on holiday, then; that you were in the Lake District with your brother, I believe.'

'It was very wrong of me to lie to you that day over luncheon,' she admitted. 'I suppose I got flustered. But I did not want my colleagues to know about it. I intended to tell you the truth afterwards, I do hope you believe that.' She looked at me earnestly.

I suggested politely that she explained exactly what had transpired.

'I never intended to go to the Lakes this year. My brother knew that. I told him that I had business in town that I wanted to settle. It was true.' Her hands played with the spaniel's ears. 'I'd been putting it off, you know, the way one does. The specialist gave me — ' She stared at me unseeingly, her grey eyes wide. 'He confirmed my own observations on the subject.' Her fingers smoothed the dog's bony forehead. 'As soon as the results of the examination were through, the X-rays and so on, I came back here. There was nothing to keep me in town, and I felt I wanted to be home. That was Sunday.

'In the evening, I rang little Nancy Royd, and told her that I had come back earlier from my holiday, as I had not been very well. She knew vaguely, I think, that I had not been really well for some time. I asked her not to tell anyone; I stressed that point. Then she said she wanted to see me, and we made an appointment for the next day. That's all. I lied to you because I couldn't bear the idea of all those people knowing and — and watching me, however sympathetically. They might even want me to resign.' She grimaced at the idea, then smiled faintly.

I was filled with admiration for this plain, elderly woman, facing death as a decent, well-bred Englishwoman should.

'Were there any other points you wanted to ask me?' she said.

I was grateful to her for her poise. Her

motherly, capable tact would put nervous young girls at their ease; certainly she would have a deft hand with an awkward situation. I guessed that the majority of her patients adored her.

'Thank you, Doctor. Just a few more points . . . Do you remember at what time Mrs. Royd arrived? About twenty-five past ten. I see. And was this just a friendly visit? Oh, professional. Did you always treat her? I see; so there was nothing at all unusual in the visit. She looked a very healthy young woman to me.'

'She is healthy,' laughed Dr. Fortescue. 'Why don't you ask me what you want to know straight out? Yes, she's going to have a baby.'

Then I remembered what had been puzzling me. It was Nancy Royd's superb calmness and placidity. At the back of her eyes one sensed a tremendous feeling of release, of relief, such as I have often seen in the eyes of a sick person after an acute pain has been vanquished.

'Poor little thing!' I said. 'What fearful bad luck to lose her husband at a time like this! She must be a plucky child: she's certainly pulling herself together most nobly.'

Dr. Fortescue was staring out of the window. 'She's a dear, brave child,' she said. 'I don't think it will prove to be such a disastrous blow to her. I do not think they were altogether happy. He was a strange man, to say the least of it.'

'Did you know him at all well?' I asked.

'No. I never could agree with his methods and theories, Mr. Chaos; in fact, I disapproved of them. He knew it, and it riled him.' She laughed. 'Of course, he had to give me the civility due to my sex, age and professional experience, albeit reluctantly.'

'He was impatient?'

'Not exactly,' she demurred. 'He believed in deep analysis, you know. He thought light therapy did more harm than good.' She shrugged and slid the dog off her knees. 'Sometimes analysts can't divorce themselves from their work: they live it; they have no external reality. I don't need to tell you that that is a bad thing — and dangerous. Dangerous for a man to dwell on the power — a power far greater than you laymen realise — that he has over other human minds. He really has complete power to mould those minds in any shape or direction he chooses. It's rather a terrible thought, isn't it? A tremendous responsibility. Enough to make a man — unless he was properly devout — feel like God, eh?' She suppressed a shudder and walked over to the window. The pale sunlight silvered her grey hair, and she turned to me with a smile. 'But who could not believe in God on a day like this?'

Again I felt that wave of admiration for her. I said, 'And, of course, some of his patients must think he is God anyway. Mmm! A nasty business. Have you any ideas yourself, Doctor, as to who might have committed the crime?'

I saw her eyes fill with tears. 'I really have no idea. I only know that it wasn't I — I can't vouch for anyone else.'

I thought I was tiring her and rose to go. Before I left, I asked her for the name of the specialist in town, the club where she had stayed, and her brother's name and address.

Thoughtfully, I strolled towards the hospital, my eye absently fixed on that monstrous piece of architecture with its ramparts and turrets thrusting above the trees.

Dr. Crawford came across a lawn with a light, swinging step. 'Why, Mr. Holmes,' she said, reproachfully, 'where have you been?'

'My dear Watson,' I said, raising a sarcastic eyebrow, 'if you had scrutinised the heel of my left boot with a little more attention, you would have remarked that there adheres to it a trifle of that yellowish clay only to be found on the far side of the valley, and — '

'I've often thought,' she interrupted, 'that the only thing that prevented poor Watson from throwing a boot at his head was Holmes's extraordinary proficiency with firearms. Well, any luck this morning? Was Nancy Royd helpful? Or mustn't I ask those questions?'

'The poor kid's going to have a baby. Isn't it tragic?'

'Yes, it's a pity,' she said.

'Did you know?' I was surprised. 'I thought Dr. Fortescue — I don't know, something she said made me think it was only diagnosed on Monday.'

'Dr. Fortescue! But she wasn't here on Monday,' she cried.

'You must try not to jump to conclusions, Watson. Which reminds me that I want to interview the rest of Royd's patients. And I'd like your advice about who's who, and whether I'd get the best results from a straight interview or a casual floating into conversation. Gresly, I know how to handle, and I'll see him later. Martin, we've done. Brace, I suppose, is still secluded? Who else have we? Ah, the fascinating Miss Gellibrand. Mmm, well; she's given me an alibi, she could be left on one side till later. Mr. Davies, now. What's he like?'

'He's a nice-looking old gentleman, suffering from senile neurasthenia. I should think you'd do best in a straight interview. Though even then, I doubt if you'll do much with him. I don't think he'd remember it if he had murdered someone on Monday.'

'Sounds jolly. And Mrs. Harrison?'

She frowned. 'She's a curious creature . . . in my opinion, she's more trouble than she's worth. She's one of those maddening people who automatically become the centre of disturbances wherever they go. If she's in a good mood, I daresay an interview would be best, though I don't know that casual conversation . . . she's very much at the hub of things, and likely to have all the gossip. I'll point her out to you. Let us walk toward the Occupation House; they'll be coming out soon, and she is sure to be among them. Who else have you?'

'Mr. Green and Mr. Croft.'

'Oh, Green, you'll like him. A dear soul, he was an Empire builder, and shouldered too much of the white man's burden. A personality conflict. As for Croft, he's a horrible type, a thorough young blackguard: you'll do best with a stiff interview. I've taken him over now, and I can help you there if you like. Look, do you see that red-headed girl with those two men? That's Mrs. Harrison.'

A thin young woman with a cap of

red-gold hair came towards us.

'Come on, Boney,' she was saying, 'let's be really dashing and stagger down to the local. I could just take a drink to my bosom right now, after that soul-destroying bit of basket-work.'

'Good morning,' said Dr. Crawford, brightly official.

'Good morning, Doctor,' they chorused, a trifle uneasily.

'Could you manage a new boy?' She pushed me forward gently.

'The more the merrier.' Mrs. Harrison gave me a warm smile. 'Meet the boys,' she said with beaming nonchalance.

We fell into step, and passed on down the drive and out of sight of Dr. Crawford's malicious smile.

# 8

## 'That is the Missing Key'

I decided that I liked Barbara Harrison. Somewhat abrupt, but a vivid personality and benevolent attitude made her a stimulating companion, in spite of her illness.

She arranged that I should sit at her table. She sat at a table for six and insisted on pushing up to make room for me. A tiny maid brought plates full of some nameless vegetarian horror, with a square of sodden green vegetable beside it. Mrs. Harrison conversed brilliantly to the table in general on erudite subjects. A flat-faced, expressionless woman opposite me burst quietly into tears. No one paid any attention. A tall, thin, anxious man fled down the length of the room, leaving a faint trail of cutlery and glass behind him — a terrific draught of wind, a door slammed, and he was gone . . . 'Good old

Smithers,' someone called loudly. And still the clatter and chatter continued as though nothing was happening.

'What a nut-house,' remarked Mrs. Harrison bitterly; and then, 'For God's sake, Miss Browne, stop snivelling into your rice pudding. Do make up your mind whether you want to eat or cry.' She whispered to me that she hadn't meant to speak so sharply; it was a swine's trick, but really it was the only thing to do. Miss Browne, however, had obediently blown her nose, dried her eyes, pulled on a pair of white kid gloves, and returned to her pudding.

Mrs. Harrison turned to me. 'Who's your doctor, by the way? Crawford? That bitch! Still, you can always get a transfer, as soon as the the new doctor comes. We — ' She broke off and stared at me earnestly for some minutes, and then burst into laughter.

'My God, this place must be giving me atrophy of the brain. You don't want coffee, do you? Let's get the hell out of here. The billiard-room will probably be empty at this hour.' She led the way.

She eyed me wistfully. 'Maybe I shouldn't have spoken,' she said. 'Would you have felt happier if I hadn't let you know that I guessed?'

'No. It just shows how bad I am at my job.'

'You're only joking, aren't you? I suppose you tagged on to me because I was one of Poison Ivy's patients. And I thought it was my well-known charm.'

'Poison Ivy?'

'I *called* him that because I was allergic to him. He used to positively bring me out in a rash. He was a bastard, my dear; he was, really.' She smiled at me confidentially. 'Still, I didn't kill the wretch. I was occupating, and before that breakfasting in bed and getting up and bathing and so on. I daresay someone would remember if they'd seen me running round in my nightie brandishing a revolver or — By the way, how was he killed?'

'With the poker,' I said, tapping my head solemnly.

She turned very pale and leant back in her chair. 'I hadn't thought about it properly before. I hadn't thought of it as — violent.' I saw that her underlip was trembling, 'This smells as if it was done by one of — us.'

'Not necessarily. No one who commits a murder is properly balanced. And possibly someone was banking on us thinking just like you, and presuming that it must have been done on impulse by a homicidal half-wit.'

'All the same — ' She gave an unhappy little laugh. ' — it's far more reasonable to suppose it was a patient than a nurse, or servant, or one of the other doctors.'

'Or an outsider,' I supplemented. 'Have you any idea who could have committed the crime?'

'Plenty of people *could* have,' she said, dejectedly. 'I could have myself. I've wanted to hit him or throw something at him when he's been particularly tiresome.'

'Have you ever done so?'

'Actually, no. Lots of them have, though, even though it's absolutely against the rules. I remember how sometimes in the winter Poison Ivy would be making up the fire, and off his guard for a few minutes — I think he trusted me that way, which only made temptation harder to overcome, for it would have been such a shock to him — and he'd stoop over the fire, presenting an absolutely superb target for my foot.' She sighed reminiscently.

'Very noble of you to be so self-controlled. Seriously, though, do you know of any of his patients who did attack him?'

'One or two. Most of them have left.' She hesitated. 'The only one that I've actually seen attacking him who is here now is Miss Brace. I don't suppose you've seen her; she's ill just now.' She jumped to her feet. 'Lord, I shall be late for my appointment.'

'Who's your doctor now?'

'McIvor, but I feel he means to turf me out just as soon as he decently can.' She ran a comb through her smooth hair and flicked a powder puff over her face.

'Do you like him?'

She shrugged. 'They're a lousy crew, skipper, they ought all to be dumped overboard.' At the door, she turned back to wave a vaguely conspiratorial hand as she drifted out.

I strolled through the communicating-doors into the squash-court. Boney and another man were playing ping-pong. Boney overdrove, and the other man grovelled about on the floor, muttering to himself in his search for the ball.

'We were only having a knock-up,' said Boney. 'Care to take over?'

The other man stood up with the ball, and I recognised him as he shouted, 'Take my bat, sir. Hullo, I saw you this morning, didn't I? That tree bloody nearly caught you, didn't it? I say, Boney, this chap nearly walked right under a tree. What's your name, sir? Green's my name.'

I introduced myself.

Green shouted, 'Chaos, eh? Funny name. You a new chap? What's wrong with you?'

'Now, Green, you know that's not allowed,' Boney said reprovingly. He turned to me. 'It's one of the rules here that patients are absolutely forbidden to discuss their ailments. The one who talks makes it worse for himself by dwelling on it. Then, too, it puts an unwarrantable strain and responsibility on the one who listens . . . '

My attention wandered to Green who was softly clapping his hands and muttering to himself in a distracted manner. I hoped Boney wasn't going to leave me alone with him.

' . . . it saves an awful lot of trouble, so I thought I'd better tell you,' he concluded. 'And now, how about a little knock-up?'

'Do carry on,' I said. 'I only came in here out of curiosity. Trying to get the lay of the land, you know. Where does that door lead to?' I pointed to the soundproof communicating door on the other side of the room.

'Oh, that leads to Dr. — to one of the doctors' consulting rooms,' said Boney casually.

'A doctor's room? Funny idea to have a door there. Is it ever used?'

Green jerked up his head and bellowed, 'Yes, it is used. I've used it myself. I was late for an appointment — I'd been playing billiards, and I came through here as a short cut. I don't believe we're supposed to use it, though; the old boy looked rather surprised when I came through.' He chuckled and lapsed into his desperate muttering once more, rubbing his hands briskly together.

I strolled across and pretended to examine the door with vague interest. I turned the handle. 'When did you come through here, Green?' I called. 'It's locked now, anyway. Are you sure you didn't dream it?'

He laughed. No, he was sure about it because he'd been playing billiards and was late in consequence. At last he remembered who he'd been playing with: young Christie — who, it appeared, was the muscular young man I had encountered at the tree-felling incident. So gradually he arrived at the conclusion that it must have been about a week ago. I expected anyway that this Christie bloke would be able to verify that. I manoeuvred the conversation round to Royd. He thought he had some funny ideas, but was really an awfully decent fellow. It appeared that Green was not yet aware of his death. He had just taken it for granted that he was away sick, I suppose. Obviously it wasn't going to be much good pumping him. I made some excuse and eased out.

I turned up a staircase hopefully, and was soon cruising aimlessly along labyrinthine corridors. Suddenly I heard a sharp wail, and someone cried in a voice pierced with anguish, 'No, no! For God's sake, leave me alone.'

The corridor turned at a right angle here, and I poked my head cautiously round the corner. A fine, athletic-looking type of girl seemed to be trying to run straight up the wall; she was clawing at it in a frantic way and moaning. Beside her stood a sister with one of those napkin affairs tied on her head. She was saying, in a voice both saccharine and astringent, 'Now, Miss Wylie, come along at once, please. I shall have to speak to your doctor if you don't behave properly, and then you'll get sent away to where you can't run loose about the place screaming your head off. Now, come along, before I lose all patience.' She put out her hand to take her by the arm as she spoke.

The girl, who was still apparently trying to get away from her by creeping up the wall, and had never stopped moaning and shuddering, now shrank back still further and said in a high-pitched squawk, 'Don't touch me, don't touch me.'

As the sister's hand closed round the girl's arm, she screamed: the helplessly bestial shrieks of someone in uncontrollable pain and terror . . .

The sister tried to clap her hand over the girl's mouth to stifle them, but she wildly thrust her away and sped down the corridor towards me, still screaming.

Suddenly, Dr. Crawford appeared from nowhere and neatly blocked her path. She bent over her and murmured soothingly.

I withdrew back into the shadow and leant against the wall. That admirable woman seemed to possess the delightful faculty of always turning up when she was most needed. My face was damp with sweat and I was feeling slightly sick . . . I didn't know who was to blame, the nurse or the girl . . .

An angry voice roused me from my thoughts. I poked my head curiously round the corner once again.

The girl had vanished. And Dr. Crawford was standing in front of the sister, letting her have it with both barrels.

'What the hell do you mean by it? What possible excuse have you for your behaviour? You had no right to let her out of your sight, and you know it. I shall most certainly report you for this, Sister Hythe, it is absolutely contrary to your orders.'

With sullen gentility, she answered: 'I do not care to be spoken to in this way, Doctor. You are at liberty to report me if you choose. But I shall put in my own report about the whole incident — *with* a complaint about your attitude, Doctor. I don't consider you have any right to dictate to me about this business. Miss Wylie is Dr. Fortescue's patient, and I take my orders in regard to her from Dr. Fortescue, not from any interfering — '

'What insufferable impudence! You won't get away with this, Sister. No amount of toadying can cover a deliberate insult to your superior. And those in charge are unlikely to overlook insolence *and* neglect of duties — '

They were both of them livid and shaking with temper by this time.

Hythe was saying: ' . . . I am here to patrol the whole corridor and keep a general eye on the patients. I was not engaged to mount guard over a raving lunatic who should be in a padded cell.'

'Dr. Fortescue will be interested in your diagnosis of Miss Wylie's case,' Dr. Crawford said icily. 'That will be all, Sister. You may go.' She turned away.

I backed up the corridor, not wanting to be caught there just then. I thought: If you were a proper sleuth-hound, you'd nose around and find out what it was all about . . . Fancy little Helen letting herself go like that! Well, it was nice to know that she *was* human, after all. Somehow, I liked her all the better for that absurd exhibition . . . it made her rather endearing.

Judging the coast would be clear again by now, I continued my explorations.

Sister Hythe was sitting on a wicker chair in a funny little glass box, writing in a large red ledger. I interrupted her and explained who I was.

'I understand that you were the first person at the scene of the crime — that is, apart from the two patients,' I said.

'Yiss,' she said, primly; 'it was Miss Brace's screams that made me go along there. I didn't actually look at the — er — deceased. I really hadn't the time, with both of them to attend to.'

I fancied she sounded almost regretful. 'I think you managed wonderfully all by yourself. Because it must have been a horrible shock for you, too.'

'Oh, yiss,' she sighed.

'Do you remember where Mr. Martin was standing when you came in?' I continued to ply her with routine questions.

Oh, yiss, she thought Dr. Royd was a genius in his own line.

Yiss, she daresaid Mrs. Royd was a nice enough little woman; but not *quite* the right person, perhaps, for Dr. Royd. Not up to his intellectual level, was she? Oh, she agreed with me, as pretty as a picture; but was that *enough*? And then he wanted children. That was a great disappointment to him: married nearly four years and no sign of a family. Of course, young women nowadays just lived for pleasure and admiration . . . I felt an unprofessional twinge of pity for the dead man. Had he known, at least, before he died that his ambition was about to be fulfilled at last?

'And the other doctors,' I asked, 'was he popular with them?'

It was her opinion that they were all jealous of him in one way or another. After all, he was a very brilliant man. And it was very hard for a man like Dr. McIvor to have to be under a man so much younger than himself. Not that he ever showed it; he was much too scrupulous for that . . . And Dr. Fortescue, now; never saying anything to him outright, but opposing him every way she could, and all because they couldn't agree over one another's methods. Oh, she was a sweet woman, but stubborn, you know. Dr. Chumly? Oh, too new to feel jealous or anything else, and it was his first post. Now, Dr. Ennis did like him, or *seemed* to; but then — she didn't want to make mischief; she was the last person to gossip — maybe there was more to that than met the eye. Certainly he was always very attentive to Mrs. Royd; that she *had* noticed, but more than that she was not prepared to say.

Privately, I thought that was just as well.

As for Dr. Crawford, no; she'd prefer not to say anything about her. *She* passed the limit of what anybody was supposed to put up with . . . the *injustice* . . . and her insulting attitude towards everyone, and her ungovernable temper . . . why, her patients were absolutely terrified of her, and even Dr. Royd dared not cross her, she created such a fuss . . . One would never take her for a psychiatrist. But, then, in her opinion, people like that should never be allowed to take over such responsible positions . . . You simply couldn't tell what they were liable to do next; they'd kill you as soon as look at you . . . absolutely — what was the word?

— amoral . . . But, there, she'd rather not talk about her at all, if I didn't mind . . . No, she really hadn't the slightest idea who could have committed such a terrible crime. She hadn't slept a wink since it had happened, and her nerves were completely unstrung. Poor, poor Dr. Royd . . .

I folded my tent and disappeared . . . I do dislike malice. Though no doubt she had some provocation; Dr. Crawford had certainly pitched into her.

\* \* \*

'Talk of angels . . . ' I said. 'I was just thinking about you. Tell me, Doctor, when you were at school, did they write on your reports: 'Helen is a very high-spirited girl'?'

She stared at me. 'What is this, Mr. Chaos? Are you feeling high-spirited yourself?' She took my hand in her warm, vibrant one and drew me to one side. 'You'd better come out into the air,' she said firmly. 'Now then, what is it all about?'

'I've just been listening to someone blackguarding you. As a matter of fact, they only just stopped short of slander; they almost accused you outright of murder.'

She looked taken aback. 'Who was it? A patient? You must tell me, I have a right to know.'

'It was Sister Hythe. She's got her needle into you, that's all.'

'Oh, that mischief-making old nanny-goat, eh?' She laughed. 'That doesn't surprise me, I've just given her a thorough dressing-down for neglecting a case. We almost came to blows. It's just typical of her to try and get her own back by making a lot of nasty insinuations about me. She's the authentic poison-pen type, who writes dirty anonymous letters. What did she say about me, anyway?'

I gave her the gist. She shivered, and I said, 'Look here, if we're going to walk about outside you'd better let me get you a coat.'

When I returned, she said, 'I've been thinking. All that stuff she said, there's a great deal of truth in it, only it's exaggerated. About Mrs. Royd, for instance. I don't suppose they were terribly happy, although I believe he was terribly in love with her. And anyone will tell you what rows I used to have with him. It didn't mean anything. I'm naturally quick-tempered, and I discovered even as a student that the best method for a *woman* doctor to get her own way was to give a little display of temperament. As for that slimy Hythe toad, she's plain jealous. They were both students together out in Australia, you know — oh, didn't you know he was Australian? — and possibly she was good-looking then; anyway, it seems there was some kind of an affair between them. How far it went, I don't know. If I know Maurice, I should say it went the whole way; but on the other hand, if I know Sister Hythe, she would have sat on her virginity until she had the contract signed and sealed. But I'm pretty certain that she expected him to marry her, and I guess she felt pretty sore when she didn't pull it off. Then, when he came here, I suppose it opened up the old wounds. Oh yes, she's been here about ten years, I think.'

I digested those facts in silence. Who would have suspected that that venomous woman cherished a hopeless passion for the handsome doctor?

'I should have thought — ' I frowned. ' — that if she wanted to marry him, the person to kill was Mrs. Royd.'

Dr. Crawford looked unhappy. 'My goodness, do you think that I'm accusing her now — or insinuating anything? I didn't mean for an instant . . . I was only defending myself.'

I reassured her. 'You were right to tell me. You must see that it does alter things. At least it gives us one more suspect — she knew him, and there was a motive of sorts. It might have been a case of hell having no fury like a woman scorned. What do you think?'

She agreed that it might just be conceivable, and asked me how the case was progressing.

'I'll tell you what I've got . . . In the first place, Nancy Royd faked up some rigmarole about going to see her husband on the fatal day and then changing her mind. So I went along to have a little chat, and she admitted that she had lied because she had gone to see Dr. Fortescue, who had particularly asked her not to tell anyone that she was back yet.'

'When did Mary get back? Or didn't she go away?'

'Yes, she went to town — I'm telling you this absolutely confidentially, Dr. Crawford — and returned on Sunday. She said she lied to me that day in front of you all because she particularly didn't want anyone to know. In any case, I shall verify all her business in town, and she knows that. However, she seemed to think that whoever killed Royd did a good day's work. She seemed to think he was heading for megalomania — '

'What nonsense!'

'I'm telling you what she said. She implied that he was too fond of the power he had over other people. How does that strike you?'

'Darn silly,' said Dr. Crawford firmly, 'and it doesn't sound a scrap like Mary. Certainly he had a great deal of power over his patients, we all have. But that doesn't mean to say that we all think we're Hitler. Maurice was far too much of a scientist to get cranky. Besides, being a psychoanalyst, he understood all those sorts of dangers and knew how to avoid them. He was terrifically absorbed in his work, believed absolutely in his own system and so on, but it's absurd to suggest that he was a megalomaniac.'

'Mmm. And Mrs. Royd? She puzzles me. Her amazing calmness — she looked positively relieved. Can you account for that?'

'No, how extraordinary. Perhaps she had a subconscious wish to kill him, and is relieved to find it taken out of her hands . . . '

I said quickly, 'You look half-frozen. Come down to the village and get some tea.'

'All right. But first I must go back to the hospital. There is a small account owing in the village, and I'd like to write out the cheque now and get it off my mind. It won't take a second.'

But I wasn't listening. I was staring at an elderly gentleman standing stock-still in the middle of the path, smiling and bowing courteously to the empty space about him.

'Good afternoon,' he was saying, bowing first right and then left. 'I hope I see you well?' He stepped back to let no one pass. 'I beg your pardon.'

I looked at Dr. Crawford anxiously. 'He's all right,' she said reassuringly. 'Mr. Davies,' she called as we drew abreast, 'I want you to meet Mr. Chaos.'

'How do you do?' He bowed politely. Suddenly he gave vent to a deep groan; then turned his back on me and addressed his conversation to an adjacent larch.

I waited in Dr. Crawford's consulting room, and watched her fix her tumbled hair and delicately dust her face with powder. She ran a lipstick lightly over the firm curve of her lips. Blinked at me owlishly as she polished her glasses, and replaced them on her small, almost-straight nose. Again, I wondered why she had never married. She must have had plenty of people in love with her, a good-looking woman like her. Maybe she had just never fallen in love with anyone herself —

Dr. Crawford gave a little astonished cry, and I jumped round. She was staring at the open drawer of her bureau as if a snake lay coiled in it.

'What is it?' I asked.

She picked up something and held it out to me. 'Do you know what that is?' she said, with a little nervous laugh. 'That is the missing key — the key to the connecting door of Dr. Royd's room.'

# 9

## 'I Killed Dr. Royd!'

We sat over a table in ye local tea shoppe, which happened fortunately to be almost empty.

'What do you think it means — honestly, now?' begged Dr. Crawford. 'Wouldn't you say that someone was deliberately trying to throw suspicion on me? Of course, someone might have been in a desperate hurry to get rid of it, and pushed it in there without meaning to do me any harm. It doesn't make it any better for me, though, does it? As far as you are concerned, I might perfectly easily have put it there myself, and then got scared or something — and thought that was the best way to get rid of it. Oh, damn!' she said fiercely. 'I can't help feeling it was with malice aforethought.' She snapped her fingers excitedly. 'I believe it was that old devil Hythe, I wouldn't put anything past her.'

'That is certainly a possibility,' I agreed. 'When did you last open that drawer? Could it have been as much as a week ago? Before the murder? That would make a lot of difference.'

She thought earnestly. Then: 'How foolish of me! That's the drawer I keep my cheque book in. Let's see when I last wrote a cheque ... Got it,' she said triumphantly. 'Chaply and Rogers, one pound seventeen and six, the day before yesterday. I'll show you the counterfoil when we go back.'

'All right. Don't bother about it anymore just now. I've got to go through the rest of Royd's patients today if I can. Do you think I can see Brace yet? I think you said she was under McIvor now? Look, could you persuade him that I must see the girl? Maybe give one of your famous displays of temperament?' I smiled.

'If I considered it was for the good of the hospital,' she said pompously.

'Thank you, Doctor,' I said with earnest solemnity. 'I know I can rely on you. Well, let's get back to the hospital.'

129

On my return I sent for Mr. Davies. He came in slowly and stood with his back against the door, groaning heavily. I asked him to think back to last Monday.

'I don't know what I'm doing here,' he said fearfully. 'They told me they were taking me to stay with my niece in the country. But she isn't here. I don't believe she even lives here — among all these people. I have a nice little flat in Half Moon Street, and they take me away . . . Where am I, sir?'

I begged him to come and sit down while we discussed the matter, and offered him a cigarette. He took one in his shaking old fingers and I lit it.

'I would like your opinion about the war, sir. You seem an intelligent young man — do you think these damn Germans have a chance?'

I reassured him, wondering which war he was thinking of. And again tackled him with the events of last Monday. He had had a special nurse then, it seemed, who was with him all the time. It was her duty never to leave him for an instant — so I guessed that was O.K., and it would take no time to check with her over that. Nor could I believe that that frail, unhappy old man could have engineered such a vile and brutal murder. I dismissed him as quickly as I could, and sent for Green next.

Green came in rubbing his hands together briskly. And muttering, 'This won't do, my God. It can't go on.'

He sat down, shouting his surprise at seeing me. I asked him the usual questions. In the morning he'd been cutting down a tree. He liked doing that best. Who had he been working with? The same gang: the wide man and the muscular young one. Oh yes, that reminded him, his axe had slipped and chopped a slice out of young Christie's hand. God, he'd been scared. It was all right, though. Nothing serious, just a nasty gash. And Christie had gone up to the house to have it seen to, and the other man had gone with him. Why hadn't he, Green, gone? Oh, he felt a bit sick. Silly thing for a chap like him to have to say, after all the things he'd seen in the jungle, but he couldn't stick the sight of blood.

I murmured that he must have seen plenty of blood in the jungle, wherever it was. He admitted that he had, and coped with it too. But cold-blooded blood was different somehow.

I agreed, and presently got rid of him.

Croft was shortish and of fairly stocky build. He looked coldly sensual, with an unhealthy white face and pale red-rimmed eyes. He slouched in with the insolence born of fear, and stood looking down on me contemptuously.

'Sit down,' I said curtly, jerking my thumb at a chair.

He asked me who the hell I thought I was. I told him.

He laughed. 'Oh, come to find out who bumped off mossy-face?'

'You seem to know a lot about it. Maybe you know who did it?'

He shook his head.

'Where were you when it happened?'

'I was taking some nice healthful exercise in the grounds,' he said, and his smile was full of some secret amusement.

'So you know what time it occurred?' I said sharply. 'You'd better do a little explaining, I think.'

'I don't know anything,' he stammered. 'One of the nurses told me Royd had been murdered, and it had happened in the morning. I don't know anything else about it. How should I?'

'All right, then. Have you got an alibi? Was anyone with you when you took this 'nice healthful exercise'? Or did you meet anyone?'

He'd dropped his posing now, and looked as miserable as the rat he was. 'I was not alone. But I cannot tell you who I was with.' He drew himself up heroically. 'You'll have to take my word for it that I'm speaking the truth and that I know nothing about Royd's death.'

'You'd better think again. What was this 'exercise', anyway? Petting, I suppose. Good Lord, man, surely your neck is more important than a girl's good name.'

'You are right,' he admitted. 'I was tumbling a skirt. One of the nurses, as a matter of fact. I didn't want to say anything in case she got the sack. Her name? Elsie Haggett. You're not — you're not going to question her?' He was horrified, and half-rose from his chair.

I explained that I had to get corroboration. I wouldn't frighten the girl, and I wouldn't tell anyone else.

He was rocking back and forth with his head in his hands and sweating. I felt sorry for him, though I disliked him as much as ever. I let him alone for a while then, but finally suggested that the only reasonable course for him to take was to confess the whole truth to me. If he was speaking the truth and had really had nothing to do with the murder, what had he to fear?

He gripped his hands tightly between his knees. 'I couldn't,' he said. 'Christ, I'm so bloody ashamed. I shall never be able to look her in the face again — and she's a nice girl, too.'

'You're sick,' I told him, 'that's why you're here. You — '

He stood up. 'Oh, shut up! I don't want that. Can I go now?'

He could. He did.

I found Dr. Crawford. She told me that McIvor had reluctantly consented to my seeing Miss Brace, and she could take me along to her right away.

The room was almost bare. In the high, white bed crouched a sallow-skinned, rabbit-faced creature with wide, terrified black eyes.

Dr. Crawford said, 'This gentleman wants to ask you a few questions, Miss Brace. There is nothing to be frightened about.' And she went away.

'I just want you to tell me what you remember about last Monday morning,' I said gently.

She didn't answer. Just stared at me out of her black eyes.

'Now, Miss Brace,' I said, more sternly, 'I must ask you to answer my questions. I understand that Dr. Royd used to come out of his room to fetch his next patient always. Now, on this particular day, do you remember what you were doing all that time? That would be from ten o'clock until Mr. Martin arrived at approximately ten-forty-five.'

No answer. She hid her face behind her hands.

'Come, Miss Brace, this won't do . . . What were you doing all that time?

Didn't it occur to you to knock on the door, or to verify the time of your appointment? Didn't you go to the door and see whether you could hear voices? Didn't you open the door a crack, just to see? Do you mean to tell me that for three-quarters of an hour you stood in the corridor outside his room and did *nothing*?' I was almost shouting,.

She shrank back on the pillows and peered through her fingers at me. 'I didn't notice the time,' she whispered. 'I was just thinking about what I was going to say in my interview.'

'I see. Did you look forward to your interviews, then? Did you find Dr. Royd helpful?'

She looked up and laughed harshly. 'Helpful! What did he care about helping people? Their suffering didn't mean a thing to him: all he cared about was his own fool notions. He liked to sit there like a kid pokes an animal in a cage, and watch your 'reaction', as he called it.' She was excited now. 'You don't know what it was like to be in that man's power, so that he could torture you.' Her voice dropped.

'I ought not to talk like that,' she said, sullenly. 'He did his best. And he helped me a lot, really. You mustn't pay any attention to me. I'm crazy.'

'Yes, but why did you stay with him if he was so awful?'

'I don't know,' she moaned.

'You can't have liked him.'

'Liked him! I hated him! Sometimes I could have killed him.'

'Did you?'

She flung the bedclothes from her in a startled gesture, and looked at me for the first time as if she really saw me. She looked as if she was going to scream or jump clean out of the window.

I felt a qualm and leapt to the door in search of assistance. Instinct made me half-turn. I felt rather than saw something whizz towards me. Before I could dodge, it hit me, catching me on the edge of my left shoulder and rebounding to the floor. A pottery lampstand lay shivered to fragments, its shade crumpled, still trailing its length of flex.

Miss Brace whimpered, 'I didn't mean to do it,' and burst into tears.

My shoulder ached, and I was furious. I remembered, however, that Martin had been at his best after his crying fit, so I hung on grimly and waited for the flow to dry up.

She showed no signs of ceasing, so I went to the door and looked up and down the corridor for a nurse. A thin, horse-faced woman skimmed by, and I stopped her and outlined the situation briefly.

'You won't get anything else out of her now,' she said. 'She'll go on like that for hours.' She sounded bored and contemptuous.

I explained that I did not like to leave her like that. Would she take over and keep an eye on her?

She would, she said indifferently, and walked past me into the room and shut the door.

After dinner, in the main lounge, Miss Gellibrand dived down on me as a falcon swoops on its prey. 'My de-urr, where have you been? I've been keeping an eye open for you. I just love to make friends with the new ones, to give them confidence right away, My family doctor said to me, 'Miss Gellibrand, you are so unselfish and you have so much poise, I just don't understand how you have a breakdown at all'.' She beamed at me triumphantly. 'But there, I've had so much trouble that I wonder I'm alive at all. Right now, while I'm sitting here talking to you, my inside is just opening and closing.'

'But you're getting better, aren't you?'

'Certainly I am,' she said stoutly. 'At least, I was, but I've lost my doctor.'

'Was he good?'

Before she had time to answer, a voice called, 'Hullo there,' and I turned to see Mrs. Harrison, austere and brittle in black, smiling down at me.

'Well, Jelly, always after the men, eh? And the handsome ones, too. You ought to be ashamed of yourself.'

Miss Gellibrand was blushing horribly, and now her blue eyes filled with tears. 'Barbara Harrison,' she said, indignantly, 'you have no right to call me that. I don't think your own conduct is any above reproach. The way you go on is a public scandal — oh!' Tears streaming, she hurried out of the room.

Barbara was laughing with amusement. I cursed her politely for having come at just that moment when I hoped I was going to get something from Gellibrand. She sobered up and apologised.

'I'm a fool,' she said contritely. 'I thought it would be funny to razz that poor old hen. Now she's gone upstairs to have a good cry, and she'll tell the whole sad story to her doctor, who will probably tell it to my doctor, and — one more black mark smirching my fair name.' She stood up. 'Look here, I'm going to do penance; it's the least I can do. I'm going up now to stem her flood of tears and listen to her tale of woe, and at the same time I'll see what I can do for you in that direction. I'll see if I can find out how she felt about Royd and so on. Women in confidence, you know . . . And I've always rather hankered to play detective.'

'Only it isn't play,' I reminded her sternly.

'All right, sweetheart, don't be petulant. I've said I'm sorry and promised to do my best.' She whirled away.

The Occupation Officer, who looked as if she ought to be a vet, rang a little bell and announced that a headdress competition was about to take place. Competitors were given fifteen minutes in which to devise a headdress of any kind out of anything they chose. She rang the bell again as a signal of dismissal, and with little shrieks and spurts of laughter the patients jostled one another from the room.

Several of the older patients, mostly men, remained behind, completely uninterested in these puerile amusements. In one corner, Gresly was playing chess with a fair-haired man. I strolled over. The game was fairly advanced, and stood at the moment in the fair-haired man's favour. Gresly exposed a rook to check the king.

The fair-haired man said, 'My dear boy, you really should not do things like that. It's tempting providence.'

'But I adore tempting providence,' said Gresly, in an acidulated voice. 'Ask the gentleman spying over my left shoulder.'

He turned to me with a pleasant smile. 'Do you play chess?'

'I know the moves.'

'We must have a game together,' he said, suddenly cheerful. 'You remember, after our game of billiards you said there would be other games.'

'Nothing I would like better.'

The first competitors were drifting down in their headdresses, and I moved off to survey them. There were several ingenious attempts, many unenterprising, and a few attractive. A blonde cutie with a silver-paper top-hat perched aloft her curls aped Marlene Dietrich. I could see three or four turbans of varying effectiveness, and a couple of bandits or pirates, impossible to tell which. Green capered absurdly as a white-faced clown. I recognised Croft sliding by as an Apache. Barbara Harrison — a few wisps of hair straggling down from under a man's cap, as a ridiculous charlady — came into the room dragging Miss Gellibrand by the arm. Miss Gellibrand was wearing a hat made from an inverted purple needlework-bag, looped beneath her chin with a tape measure that tied in a coquettish bow under her left ear.

They all lined up for the march past. The little 'vet' struck up 'El Relicario' on the piano and they trotted round the room. Each time they came round, Miss Gellibrand fastened me with her bright blue eye in a determined sort of way. I wondered what Barbara had got out of her — if anything. The fourth time round, she broke rank and hurried over to me.

'Mr. Chaos,' she begged, 'I've just *got* to speak to you, it's vurry important. Where can we be alone? Maybe the Silence Room will be empty . . . ' She pulled me out of the room.

The Silence Room was empty, and she pushed me inside, shut the door, and leant against it, her bosom heaving tumultuously

She looked me straight in the eye. 'Mr. Chaos, *I* did it. I killed Dr. Royd! I just had to confess. When I saw you looking at me in that *piercing* way, I just felt you *knew* my guilty secret, and I just *had* to confess.' She gazed at me expectantly.

I suggested that we both sat down. 'Do you usually kill people you love?' I asked, lightly.

'Oh! Mr. Chaos, don't jest,' she moaned reproachfully. 'If you only knew how I *loved* that man.'

'And did he reciprocate your affection?'

'Sometimes, I think he did. He wasn't happy with that foolish little wife of his . . . Once he said, 'Do you ever think about how *different* things would be if I were free?' And another time, I remember, he said, didn't I think that the most passionate woman was one who had never had a chance to express it? And then, when I was explaining a symptom to him, how I get a kind of a stifling feeling at the pit of my stomach, he suggested I was love-hungry. I said, 'Put your hand here, Doctor, and feel.' And he said, 'Why, do you want me to *lose control* of myself, Miss Gellibrand?' Ah, I'm a woman of the world, Mr. Chaos. A man doesn't say a thing like that unless he *means* something by it.'

'I still don't understand why you killed him.'

'That would be beyond your comprehension. The dark places of the soul, my de-urr, the dark places that are hidden to all but the few. Not many souls exist that go into those terrible depths and come out again. But those that do come back *purified*; yes, *purified*. So, you see, I loved him, and I killed him that I might be purified by the experience.'

'All right, Miss Gellibrand, playtime's over for today. Where did you get the revolver from to shoot him?' I barked. She hesitated uncertainly.

'You shot him, didn't you? You must know where you got the gun from,' I shouted, like a P.I. in a movie. 'Out with it! Where did you put the gun afterwards? Where'd ya hide it?'

Something had gone wrong somewhere, the scene had side-slipped somehow; I could see that she just couldn't figure out what had happened.

'Well,' she said nervously, backing to the door, 'well . . . '

The door opened and Sister Hythe poked her napkin-enfolded head round the door, 'What,' she demanded in tones of frozen gentility, 'is going on here? Don't you know that this is the *Silence* Room? For people who wish to be *quiet*.'

I explained to Sister Hythe that there had only been the two of us, surely it didn't matter if there was no one else.

'That has nothing to do with it, Mr. Chaos,' she snapped, 'No one is allowed to talk here. It's a rule of the establishment. There are plenty of public rooms in the house if you wish to talk . . .'

Miss Gellibrand, looking absurdly like the Red Queen with the purple bag at a rakish angle over her forehead, drew herself up with great dignity. 'Then maybe *you* had better stop talking, Sister, and then silence will once more reign supreme.' She bowed to me, said, 'Good evening, Mr. Chaos,' and sailed out of the room.

# 10

'Had a Pleasant Evening Spying?'

That night, when I got back to The Three Crows, I went straight upstairs to my room, poured myself a drink, and lay down on the bed with a pencil and pad. I considered the moment had arrived to clear my head with a 'Bradshaw.' Patients first, I thought.

*GRESLY.*

I wrote. And underneath:

*Motive.* He hated him like hell and was afraid of him, of being so much in his power, afraid because he knew too much. (But was there anything *to* know?)

*Opportunity.* He had an appointment he said he never kept. But supposing really he started out for a walk and then crept back unseen — Royd would naturally be waiting for him and let him in — he only needed to bang him on the head and creep away again . . . through the squash-room door. He had a clear half-hour in which to work that trick, and no alibi for the time in question.

*Probability*. Not very high. Faints at the sight of blood. Exaggerates his feelings, and is a typical neurotic. Has a violent temper, but I should judge he lacks the nerve for a premeditated crime.

*MARTIN*.
*Motive*. More or less as Gresly.
*Opportunity*. Unless he could have known that Gresly had missed his interview and somehow gone in then and assassinated Royd, he had no opportunity. He did not kill him when he discovered the body, because when McIvor arrived on the scene a few minutes later the blood was already coagulated.
*Probability*. Low. See Gresly.

*GREEN*.

*Motive*. None so far. He thought him a jolly good fellow.

*Opportunity*. Was left alone for some time in the beech wood not far from Royd's windows. He's a strong, husky chap, and probably could just have made it.

*Probability*. Low. He seems not to realise his death even. Sickens at the sight of blood. On the other hand, he's batty as a coot and probably capable of anything.

*DAVIES*.

*Motive*. Zero.

*Opportunity*. Zero.

*Probability*. Zero.

*CROFT*.

*Motive*. None so far.

*Opportunity*. Zero.

*Probability*. Zero, except that he's a nasty bit of work.

*HARRISON*.

*Motive*. As Gresly, Martin, etc.

*Opportunity*. None so far. Though she might have been able to slip unseen from the Occupation House.

*Probability*. Low. Unlikely to lose her temper to the extent of murdering him on impulse, and although she is capable of working out a premeditated plan, I do not believe that she has the physical strength to have wielded that poker.

*BRACE.*

*Motive*. Same as usual, I guess.

*Opportunity*. She had three-quarters of an hour clear. Her absence from the passage would not even have been remarked.

*Probability*. Pretty high. Violent temper, throws things. Was known to have attacked Royd on more than one occasion. On the other hand, knowing this, would Royd have let her get behind him with a poker nearly as big as herself? And is she mentally capable of playing a part with Martin afterwards for quarter of an hour? She was the only one to be absolutely prostrated with shock.

*GELLIBRAND.*
*Motive.* She lurved him!
*Opportunity.* None. Her alibi is
O.K. and checks with the others.
*Probability.* Zero.

Well, that knocked off the patients. I took
a long drink from the glass at my side,
and wrote:

*MRS. ROYD.*
*Motive.* She was, according to
reports, downtrodden. They were not
happy together. And she is not even
pretending to grieve over his death,
nor does it seem to have been a
shock. Maybe she hated him, or was
just plain sick of him.
*Opportunity.* Suppose she did go
and see her husband, after all, and
was playing double-bluff with us. She
may be in cahoots with Fortescue
over the visits to her.
*Probability.* Medium. She is about
to have a child, which tells both for

and against her. Perhaps she didn't like the father. Or wouldn't a pregnant woman instinctively take too much care of her unborn child to commit murder? Such a brutal act does not fit in with Nancy Royd's temperament. She might have instigated it, or be in cahoots with someone over it.

*McIVOR.*
*Motive.* Professional jealousy. He ought to have been Head himself. Not only was this younger man put over him, but he was wholly incompetent on the administrative side, and the place was on the downgrade. McIvor has the interests of the hospital very much to heart.

*Opportunity.* Not much, unless he lingered behind on some pretext when the others dispersed to their separate rooms, and that would be pretty risky, unless he *knew* that Gresly was going to play truant.

*Probability.* Medium. He disliked and disapproved of Royd. I can't imagine McIvor getting behind a man and smashing his head in such a messy way; but a psychiatrist is not likely to make that sort of slip, and he might have reckoned that I would think that very thing. Why was he never made Head, in spite of his seniority and apparent suitability? What was there against him?

*ENNIS.*
*Motive.* None apparently.
*Opportunity.* None apparently.
*Probability.* Practically zero. He didn't seem to care for him, but what of it? Seemed to think plenty of people might have murdered him with good reason. Could he possibly have left his patient at Garrangarth, raced back, killed Royd, and then gone back to Garrangarth in time to pick up his patient again? Investigate possibilities there.

*CHUMLY.*
*Motive.* Zero.
*Opportunity* No alibi. Could easily

have walked in and killed him without anyone noticing his presence. Especially as, if Gresly did leave the hospital grounds, he must have passed his cottage.

*Probability*. Rather low. Very new to the place, and unlikely to have worked up an uncontrollable passion. Unless he is in love with little Nancy Royd. Maybe they worked together over it, or maybe she dominated him and persuaded him to do it for her sake. Consider that possibility. That would rate him fairly high.

*FORTESCUE*.
*Motive*. She disapproved of him strongly. Thought he was suffering from megalomania. Believed he was totally unsuitable for Nancy, of whom she was very fond.

*Opportunity*. Time enough before Nancy arrived, again provided she knew Gresly was safely out of the way.

*Probability*. Medium. Would she

154

have chosen such a filthy method? It's such a very unladylike way of killing a person. She knows she is going to die in a few months anyway, maybe she was prepared to take the risk of being found out. She may have looked on it as fundamentally a good action. But she is a religious woman. There is something a trifle fishy about her trip to town to see the specialist and then coming back without letting anyone know. Except Nancy Royd; she knew.

I hesitated a moment and then continued writing.

*CRAWFORD.*
*Motive.* None. All the same, like everybody else — no liking for him.
*Opportunity.* Same as for McIvor or Ennis.
*Probability.* Low. She admitted to violent temper, but probably far more controlled than she allowed it to be supposed, since she acknowledged that she used her rages for her

own advantage. Was known to have frequently quarrelled with Royd over professional matters. And the key to the squash-court was in her desk (for what that is worth). On the other hand, I can't believe she could commit such a clumsy crime even on impulse, and a premeditated crime is highly improbable with so slight a motive.

Rather as an afterthought, I wrote:

*HYTHE*.
*Motive*. Unrequited love? Or rage at having been thrown aside — like a worn-out orange or a sucked glove, as they say.
*Opportunity*. She couldn't have an alibi for the time, as she was on duty, and therefore trotting about the hospital. That left her a fair amount of opportunity to slip in unnoticed.
*Probability*. Medium. An unpleasant, malicious woman, but that does not make her a murderess, of course. But she probably knows more about

Royd than anyone, since they were students in Australia.

Supposing Royd, who seems to have had a curious desire to have people in his power, was blackmailing Hythe? Knew something about her in the old Australian days? Second motive for murder, possible even stronger than first. Investigate. M'Caley could cover the Australian angle.

I poured myself another drink and leant back on the pillows to re-read the script. It had washed out Davies and Croft, and that was something. And Green was practically out of it too.

If I only knew whether it was on impulse or premeditated. The person who could kill in that way impulsively was hardly likely to do so with forethought. Anyhow, if it was premeditated, the plan was conceived and executed with hideous cunning and implied brains and subtlety, the whole point being that it should *appear* to be impulsive. In the circumstances, it seemed far more likely to be an impulsive crime. And the most impulsive people were the patients, with Miss Brace high on the list.

At least the hospital officials would be pleased; it won't raise nearly so much of a stink. They could probably arrange for her to be quietly transferred to Broadmoor. I pulled myself up sharply. I had still to get proof. Maybe I could get a confession out of her. Next time I would take Dr. Crawford with me, and then I wouldn't get in such a jam. She knew how to handle these people. I wondered how she would look on Brace as a murderess — from a psychiatrist's point of view. Or there was Gresly. He had the same opportunity as Brace. In fact, I would have liked to go over the whole list with Dr. Crawford, except for the fact that her name was among those present. But she'd understand that one had to be strictly honest, because it was much the same in her profession too. She was a grand woman, and if she could help me on the psychological side with my 'Bradshaw', it should tidy things up quite a bit. I wondered whether she believed it to be a crime of impulse or premeditation. I had never thought to ask her.

I looked at my watch. Eleven-thirty. I felt hot and restless, and I knew that I was in for a haunted night. I leant out of the window and breathed in the stock-scented air. A pleasant walk . . .

I donned a heavy turtle-necked sweater, pulled on a pair of running shoes, grasped my torch, and crept quietly down the old oak stairs. I gently slid back the bolts on the casement windows in the parlour, dropped out onto the lawn, and closed them softly again behind me.

Without deliberate thought, I turned up the road towards the hospital. Of course, everyone would be in bed there too.

The moon was just on the wane and its cold light was flooding the countryside. I wondered if there was anything in the old wives' tale that the moon affected lunatics. Probably.

I had reached the crest of the hill by now, and the hospital stood out as black as a cardboard palace against the moon.

There was something unreal about it.

I swung into the drive, avoiding the gravel and treading on the noiseless turf. The moon swung with me, beating its beams in vain against the blindly staring windows. Not a sign of life. I stared at this black-and-white cinematic background . . . Yes, that was all it was, a background . . . background to a murder . . .

Resolutely, I turned my back on the hospital and hastened my footsteps towards the spinney. An owl hooted longingly. It was dark in the spinney, and I paused to accustom my eyes to it, for I did not wish to use my torch. I knew that on the far side an ancient yew hedge led to a secret garden. No, it was too black. I could never see my way through the spinney. There might be rabbit holes or goodness knew what. I had no wish to break my neck or an ankle. I turned to go back, and as I did so, distinctly heard a high-pitched voice say huskily, 'Oh, what's the use of going over it again . . . '

I stopped and held my breath. Where had that come from? 'Why blame me?' it said fretfully. "'T'ain't my fault. Did I start any of it?'

I located it then: the far side of the spinney, in the secret garden. But who was it? Now I would get across the spinney at any cost. Cautiously, I felt my way from tree to tree. A twig snapped under my foot. I listened.

'Can't 'elp it, it's Father,' said the frigidly monotonous voice, 'I don't care one way or t'other, I'm sure. But it's Father, don't you see?'

Whether the other person was not talking, or whether the voice was too faint, I don't know. It was inaudible, anyway.

"'T'warn't no use to lie to Father, *you* know that,' said the childlike voice again. And then, after a pause: 'Reckon you'd best pay and be done with it. What's the use in saying you 'aven't got any money *now*? Easy to say that when you've had your bit of fun . . . Ow, go easy now . . . Dessay you got something you kin sell, ain't you?'

I fumbled round close to the hedge, seeking an entrance.

'Don't know why I should bother myself about it,' complained the voice. 'It's what Father says, an' 'e says that if 'e don't get the money, it'll be you-know-what for you.'

I could see the entrance now, a black gap in the moonlight a couple of yards away.

'I'll tell 'im that if you like, but 'e won't like it. You don't want 'im to turn nasty, do you . . . ?' fluted the voice.

I reached the gap. A queer, jumbled statue stood out lined blackly against the moonlit sky . . . Shapeless and twisted, it had a terrifying touch of fantasy in that eerie light . . . And then, as I watched, it quivered and broke into two . . .

'Oh God, run!' urged the taller shape, in a low, forcible voice. The little half needed no advice, and was already skimming to shelter in a clump of shadow, and on . . . out of sight . . .

The tall one stood poised opaque and slender in front of the moon, then twisted beyond me and sped toward the distant second entrance. I tore after it.

It was someone who knew the terrain

far better than I. And he was keeping well ahead of me. Suddenly, I realised my mistake. I was following his lead, and that was what he wanted me to do. I must get back to the hospital and cut off his retreat. I doubled back on my tracks . . .

I couldn't cover the whole of this damned great building. How did he propose to get in again? There must be a door or a window or something unlatched. I'd just have to go round and try to find it before he did. I pressed my hands gently against the nearest window. It didn't yield and I moved on.

A window swung away under my pressure. I threw a leg over the sill and climbed inside, stumbling against great folds of heavy velvet curtains. Cautiously, I switched on my torch. The narrow beam ran over bare walls and wavered on to the ping-pong table. The squash-court. I drew back into the shadow of the curtains and waited.

It was not long, however, before the glass swung inward. A leg appeared over the ledge. And another.

My torch flashed on. 'Good evening,

Mr. Gresly,' I said, and caught him by the arm. With his free hand, he punched me low in the stomach and I gasped, but hung on to the arm I held. I was handicapped by having the torch in my hand, and I did not care to drop it in case I could not find it again. I let go of his arm, flashed the torch in his face with my right hand, and let him have it on the jaw with my left.

He staggered and fell against the ping-pong table, which skidded noisily across the floor. He sat on the floor nursing his jaw and swearing softly. 'For God's sake, don't make such a bloody row. Do you want to wake the whole ruddy hospital?'

I picked him up. 'Hope I didn't hurt you,' I said.

'Yes, I guessed it was you,' he sneered. 'Had a pleasant evening spying?'

I sat on the sill and thought for a bit. Then: 'You know why I'm here — to investigate this murder. But I'm not the police, you know. I don't really go poking my nose into a lot of other messes — except by accident. All I want to do is to clear up my own job.'

There was silence for what seemed a long time. 'Where are you?' I said suddenly, and switched on my torch.

His slender tousled figure flickered in the beam for an instant. 'I was thinking. I suppose I had better explain everything,' he sighed. 'Of course, you realise that that was my alibi for Monday.'

'Yes. But I don't understand all the mystery. Didn't you realise you were a suspect?'

'Oh, I was terrified, but I thought on the whole that it would be easier for me to prove my innocence of the murder, if it ever came to that point, than ... I suppose really it's because this is real to me, an absolutely deadly, hopeless reality. Royd was always telling me I was incurable. If I ever wanted to get away from here — and sometimes I've felt I'd die if I couldn't get away — he always used to throw that in my face. And then I was so afraid of prison. It was either this or that. And he used to taunt and threaten me, you know ... My God, he was a beast ... And then I got so that it seemed hopeless and useless even to try to be cured . . . And afterwards, it was like cat and mouse . . . ' His voice quivered to a painful silence.

'Thanks, Gresly. I'll need that name and address for the alibi, you know. But you needn't worry about that. Blackmail is a criminal offence, you know, and it gets a pretty stiff sentence. Didn't you know that? I suppose you were afraid to use it? You've been punishing yourself. But I guess I can fix that up for you. I shouldn't worry anymore. You'd better get off to bed now, it must be nearly two. Goodnight.'

I thought I would be able to sleep now. I jog-trotted down the hill dreamily, by the setting moon. I slid back the bolts on the parlour casements and crept up to my room. My clothes dropped in a heap on the floor.

'A profitable evening's work,' I yawned. '*Though they'll none of them be missed, that's another off the list*,' I misquoted, and dark sleep caught me as I fell.

# 11

## 'I'd Rather be Down in my Nice Cool Sewer Any Day'

It was getting on for eleven o'clock when I strolled up to the hospital next morning. The sulky porter looked at me as if he had never seen me before. I asked if Dr. Crawford had come in.

'Yus, Dr. Crawford is in.'

'I'll go up,' I said, and started towards the stairs.

'Sorry, sir. I didn't know you wanted to see Dr. Crawford. She's engaged at the moment, sir, to tell you the truth. Would you like me to ring through and find out if she can see you?'

I kept my temper and nodded.

'Hullo, gennelman here to see you, Doctor.'

Squeak, squeak, said the receiver at his ear.

He jerked his little pointed chin at me

inquiringly. 'Name?' he mouthed. He repeated it into the mouthpiece after me. 'Yus . . . very good, Doctor.' He hung up. 'Dr. Crawford will see you, sir.'

Dr. Crawford's 'engagement' was with Mrs. Royd. Mrs. Royd was not looking well, pale as if she had a fever, and her eyes glittered. Dr. Crawford had her head buried in a cupboard when I came in.

'Good morning!' she cried from the depths. 'I'm just making some tea. You'll have some, won't you?' She turned round, cups dangling from her fingers. The electric kettle hissed petulantly, and she flew to attend to it.

There was an atmosphere in the room, I thought . . .

'Don't stand about all over the place,' begged Dr. Crawford. 'You're making us both nervous. Are you about to make an *announcement*? Nancy, do you take saccharine? I forget,' she chattered.

'I have some here somewhere about,' said Nancy languidly.

'No, don't use yours. I have plenty. Wait a minute.' She groped in the cupboard. 'And you?' she queried of me.

I shook my head. 'I'm sweet enough, as they say below-stairs. How's the garden?' I asked Nancy.

She smiled absently, but did not answer. I caught Dr. Crawford's eye and she shook her head at me.

I began to recount to them Miss Gellibrand's romantic confession of the night before, complete with work-bag. Dr. Crawford was amused, and Nancy Royd pretended to be, politely. I don't think she was listening entirely. Dr. Crawford plied me with questions about Gellibrand.

'That's what I meant about Harrison,' she said. 'Whenever she is around, it surely is leading to trouble. I bet you anything you like that Harrison put the idea in her head. Told her that you were a detective, for instance, and a few similar juicy tit-bits. Then the old girl mulled them around in her head for a bit, added it up, and that was the answer. That's the way of it,' she explained, looking at Nancy, not me.

Nancy Royd stood up. 'I must be going, Helen. Thank, you for the tea — and the talk. I'll think about it and let you know what I decide. As for the rest . . . ' She raised her little plump shoulders. ' . . . I shall leave it to you.'

'You can leave it to me, all right,' she assured her. 'I'll deal with it. Take care of yourself, my dear.'

I thought I saw Nancy Royd wince. Her large glittering eyes passed over me vaguely as she straightened her black felt hat in the mirror. She held out a small hand. 'Goodbye, Mr. Chaos. I expect I shall be seeing you again quite soon.'

'I hope so.' I smiled as I opened the door. 'And what,' I demanded, as I closed the door behind her, 'is the matter there? Is she suffering from delayed shock or what?'

'I don't think she's feeling any too good,' said Dr. Crawford, leaning back in her chair. The light from the window behind caught her face for the first time, and I saw that she looked tired and strained and there were dark circles under her eyes. She looked her age and rather plain, with deep lines running from nose to mouth. There was something decidedly pathetic about her as she dropped in the chair, listless with fatigue, and the very antithesis of her brightly poised self.

'Look here,' I said. 'Would you rather I went away?'

'Do I look haggish?' She groped for her compact and walked over to the window, 'Don't go,' she said. 'Tell me what you've come about . . . Go ahead, I'm listening.'

I explained to her about my 'Bradshaw', and how I wanted her to go over it with me and give me the benefit of her psychiatric experience. I rambled on . . . She made no comment, and presently I looked up from my script. Her back was to me and she was staring out of the window.

I went over to her, and saw with a painful pang of compassion that she was crying. She was biting her lips wildly in a desperate attempt to regain her self-control, and her small tawny hands were clenched.

But what was particularly heartrending to me was the utter silence in which she struggled to conquer her grief. I tried to think of something comforting to say to her. I put my arm round her shoulders.

She tensed and moved away.

'Please,' she jerked out. 'Go away . . . Leave me alone . . . I'm just being foolish . . . I'll be all right directly.'

'Not till you tell me what the trouble is. Cry if you want to, darling.'

I held her close and made meaningless, soothing noises. After a bit, she stopped, and took my handkerchief.

'There! I feel better now. I must look a perfect sight now, don't I? Let me get at that mirror . . . Oh God, how shameful! Pass me my bag, please,' she chattered on whilst she dealt with her face. 'I must say, you behaved very handsomely,' she went on, smearing her face with cold cream. 'And I haven't even thanked you for your shoulder yet.'

'Don't feel embarrassed,' I said slowly. 'I'm not going to ask any awkward questions.'

She leant her arms on the mantelpiece and stared at me earnestly in the glass. 'You're feeling hurt,' she said gently. 'I don't mind telling you what it was . . . I just thought it would be better perhaps not to talk about it, but I guess you know

172

all about it, anyway . . . It's Mary.' She wiped the grease off her face and turned to me. 'Nancy just told me — she came here to tell me. She wanted to know just what it all meant. She thought maybe I could persuade Mary to stop working and give herself a chance.'

'She won't do that,' I said, 'I know.'

She shrugged. 'I can only try,' she stared at me unseeingly. 'And then, you see, it sort of swept over me . . . Poor Mary . . . going through all that hateful, terrifying business alone . . . And, even now, wanting to keep it a secret. That's what it was.'

I knew she wasn't telling me the truth, but — well, some things are private, even a detective can see that. I let it go. I had to take it on trust that if it had had anything to do with the case she would have been honest enough to tell me, however much it hurt her. She turned and faced me. 'Most unprofessional behaviour on my part.'

'Mine, too.'

She twinkled at me. 'In fact, we have both behaved rather disgracefully. How about if we wipe the whole thing out? Is that a bargain?' She held out her hand.

I took it in mine, and said slowly, 'It is, Dr. Crawford. But I shall never cease to regret it, Helen.'

'Now,' she said briskly, polishing her glasses, 'do I look myself again?' She did. Fresh and neat. No one was likely to dream of the exhaustingly emotional morning she had spent, I assured her.

'Good. Because I am now going to visit Mary, and I must be very sure of myself and not make any mistakes.'

I tried to persuade her not to go. She'd had a trying morning. This would be at best a difficult situation to handle. Mary did not want people interfering or advising. She had told me that she was afraid that if anyone knew they would want her to resign.

'Naturally they would. It's the only thing that can help her at all,' she said calmly. 'Besides, I don't think she realises to what an extent that sort of thing affects the patients. Oh, I grant you it's unconscious, but that makes it harder to handle. No, you must let me deal with this in my own way. I am a doctor, you know.'

'All right,' I said. 'See you later, I suppose.'

'You came here to discuss something with me, and I'd completely forgotten all about it. What a rotten Watson I'm turning out to be. I can't tell you how sorry I am. Will it wait?'

'It will. And another thing. I want to tell you about Miss Brace. I've got to see her again, but I think you'd better be there this time. I made a bit of a mess of it before. But I'll tell you all about that later. So long, Watson.'

'So long, Holmes!'

When she came back after lunch, she told me that I was right. Mary would not consent to resign or take a holiday. She had asked Mary to dinner that night, however, and would I come, too? I would. Dr. McIvor was engaged already, and so was Dr. Ennis; but she had got young Chumly to make up a four. A pity she couldn't get the others; she would have liked to have a party for Mary. But this was better than nothing, and would prevent her feeling too much alone.

And now, if I liked, we could go along and tackle Brace. I outlined to her what had occurred the day before.

'I can guess it scared the blue daylights out of her when she threw the lampstand at you and it hit the mark,' she said. 'I conjecture that she'll be too scared to so much as look you in the face today. But don't take any notice of that.'

Miss Brace didn't look at me. She was lying flat on her back in bed when we came in, staring at the ceiling.

We greeted her politely, but without getting any response. Dr. Crawford made a face at me. 'Let's sit down, anyway,' she suggested.

'You remember me, Miss Brace.' I said, persuasively. 'I'm the gentleman you threw the lamp at yesterday. I've come back to tell you not to worry about it. I'm not the least bit angry, only sorry that I upset you. Please forgive me.' I paused. The blank black eyes continued to stare unblinkingly at the ceiling. 'I want to ask you a few questions. Miss Brace, did you go into the room with Mr. Martin? Or did you go in afterwards?'

She wouldn't play. Cursing heartily inside, I passed the buck to Dr. Crawford.

'Why don't you let go of your grief about Dr. Royd's death?' she suggested. 'Don't bottle it up, let it go, Miss Brace. What is worrying you? Are you ashamed of having loved him, perhaps?'

Miss Brace sat upright abruptly. 'How did you know?' she whispered, her black eyes furtive with fear. 'You've been spying on me. I know there is a hidden microphone system all over this place, so that you can spy on everyone.' Her rustling voice died away.

Dr. Crawford signalled to me to be quiet.

The dry whisper restarted: 'Spying . . . they're all jealous . . . they want to make trouble . . . get something against me . . . They're trying to frighten me now, pretending you're dead . . . It isn't true. I won't believe it. Then it won't be true . . . you wouldn't leave me, would you, darling? It's her; she's trying to make me believe you're dead, so that I'll leave you alone . . . Then she can have you . . . I'm not so crazy, you know that . . . I'll see she doesn't get you, darling.' She gave a little snivelling laugh.

I looked at Helen pleadingly. Did I have to listen to this? She was making rapid notes on the back of an old envelope. 'All right.' She smiled. 'I'll handle this. I understand it. You go and cool off.'

I needed no second bidding. Outside, I almost broke into a run. Faugh! The whole thing became more revoltingly obscene every day. I couldn't stick much more of it.

I leant against the iron bar that divided the landing window and stuck my head out. Far below, foreshortened to a grotesque dwarf, Barbara Harrison walked between two men, brandishing a golf-club. One of them must have made some teasing remark to her, for she suddenly leapt forward, shaking it violently at him in mock anger. I presumed it was mock anger from the faint tinkle of laughter that drifted up to me. I withdrew my head wearily.

Dr. Crawford swept towards me with her light, rapid tread.

'I was just wondering how you doctors can stick it, year in, year out,' I said. 'I suppose it demands a special type of mind, but for my part I'd rather be down in my nice cool sewer any day.'

'Don't be so stupid,' she said irritably. 'We're all just the same inside, only we don't have to turn ourselves inside out and face the shock of it; we can go on in our blissful little Eden of self-admiration. Whereas these poor wretches have got a sprocket jammed or something, and are stuck at some point in their lives and can't get beyond it: so we have to take them to pieces and start again. But that's no reason for putting on that disgusted, sickened air, any more than you would over a bit of machinery that had jammed and needed repairing. It's you but for the grace of God, believe me. No man may be a hero to his valet, but every man is a god to himself.'

I said meekly that I was not feeling at all like a god just then.

She laughed. 'Dear me, what an excellent subject you are for a lecture! I hope I didn't bore you, but you just happened to hit my pet hobby-horse. I always enjoy airing my views, so at least I've had some pleasure.'

'And *I* some profit.'

'Thank you. Well, now for Miss Brace. I suppose you realised before you left that the trouble was that she didn't want to face up to Dr. Royd's death because she loved him. She'd transferred the whole weight of her repressed emotions onto him — parental love, sexual love and maternal love, all rolled into a confused heap. That is a very frequent occurrence in psychotherapy, and in the ordinary course of events the physician finds suitable emotional outlets for the patient to transfer to gradually as he or she progresses. But should something untoward occur — as has occurred in this particular instance — to arrest the case at the early stages, it can be disastrous.'

'Yes, I daresay. But why all this pretence of hating him, then? Why used she to attack him?'

'I expect she was lying to herself about it; it was easier for her to bear the idea of hating him than the rather humiliating idea of unrequited love, so she would pretend that she loathed and feared him. As for when she used to attack him, she wanted to attract his attention, make him notice her. She may have hoped to arouse desire in him by bodily contact, when she fought and kicked and scratched. She was not stable emotionally,' she informed me seriously.

'You don't say,' I murmured dimly. 'Did she say anything to make you think she might have murdered Royd? Or, how do you look on it as a possibility, anyway?'

She shook her head decisively. 'That's what I've been trying to explain to you,' she said patiently. 'Even though she did hate him, it wasn't that sort of hate. You don't kill a man to attract his attention. And it's extremely unlikely that she hit him without meaning to kill him. In the first place, more than one blow was struck, wasn't it? Also, she's a feeble little creature, and I don't think she'd have taken that great heavy poker if she just meant to hurt him or frighten him. Besides, I don't think for a moment that he'd have let her get behind him; he was much too canny about that, you must remember. Is there any other thing that does not seem to you to tally?'

There wasn't. 'I'm glad the poor thing's eliminated,' I said. 'Though it's a pity, because she was one of my most eligible suspects.'

Dr. Crawford said, 'Don't talk like that . . . Oh, what is the matter with me today? I'm feeling singularly tender-hearted.'

'I'll give you till dinner tonight in which to recover and be once more your old tough self,' I admonished her. 'Meanwhile, I am off in search of Dr. McIvor.'

Dr. McIvor was seeing a patient, so I hung about and cooled my heels till he was free to see me.

'Ah, Mr. Chaos,' he said, as I came in. 'I've been expecting you.'

'Indeed, Doctor! And what can I do for you?' But it was nothing except that he had been expecting me to give him a report on the case, which I had no intention of doing — save in the briefest outline.

'I really came to see you about Dr. Royd's memorandum, or whatever you call 'em, on his patients. Would you hand them over to me, please?'

He smiled. All the files relating to old cases were kept in the cellars; the cellars were jammed from floor to ceiling with them. But, as soon as maybe, he would find them and hand them over to me.

I then asked him if he could let me have the notes on which Dr. Royd was writing at the actual moment he was killed.

'Now, let me see,' he muttered, 'where did I put it?' He began opening and shutting the drawers of his desk and turning over piles of paper in an uneasy manner. 'I put it somewhere for safety. Now, where was it?'

I was angry. 'It'll turn up again when you least expect it,' I said. 'Don't bother about it now. Perhaps you remember what was written there?'

'No,' he said. 'I never even looked.'

'Then it's absurd of me to presume that it had anything to do with you?'

He looked at me blankly. 'Why should it have, rather than anyone else?'

I shrugged. 'I thought it might have

been something to do with that little mystery concerning your Headship.'

'What exactly do you mean?'

'I mean that Royd might have found out the whys and wherefores, and was being a little tiresome about it, perhaps.'

My arrow, as aimless and hopeful as poor blind Cupid's, had struck.

His sallow skin blanched, and the corners of his mouth twitched. 'Tiresome? I'll tell you what it was. He had found out, and he wanted me to accept less money on that account. Though the salaries had nothing to do with him, all that is arranged by the Board. But he thought that could be arranged between ourselves, and I could pay the money back to the hospital through him. He had got that side of it in such a mess, you know, and he knew how I felt about the place — he was playing on that.'

'Didn't it occur to either of you that it was pretty nearly blackmail?'

'That's what I told him,' he said, banging the desk excitedly. 'But he wouldn't have it. He said that it was a purely friendly arrangement, and quite impersonal, to benefit the hospital. It wasn't true, though, because he meant to get rid of me otherwise and find someone cheaper — like Chumly. Not that I think he could have done, mind you, because all appointments go via the Board, and they wouldn't want to get rid of me unless he had something definite against me.'

'I see. And ultimately, did you agree?'

'We — we hadn't decided.'

'But in your heart, didn't you know what you intended to do?'

'I didn't mean to give in,' he admitted.

'It depended on your goodwill, then: he hadn't got anything that he could use against you?'

'No, there wasn't anything he could use against me.'

'And you didn't think it likely that he would try and fake up something in some way?'

'I didn't.'

'So it must have been rather a shock to you when you discovered that that was just what he intended to do.'

He jerked his chair back, so that it

scraped along the floor. 'What makes you think he meant to do that?' he demanded.

I opened my hands expressively. He looked away from me, gnawing a finger unhappily. There was a lengthy silence.

At last, I rose to go. 'Maybe you'll think it over,' I said. But he made no answer: just sat there stock-still, thinking, thinking . . .

# 12

## 'The Inquest! . . . I'd Quite Forgotten the Inquest'

Dr. Crawford was looking most attractive in a severely plain black velvet evening frock, ornamented with a diamond clip on the shoulder.

We were waiting for Dr. Fortescue. Chumly was twiddling alternately with the wireless and his glass of sherry. He didn't seem exactly delighted to see me, I noticed.

'Here's Mary,' said Dr. Crawford, and went to meet her as she came in. She had on a flowered blue chiffon, and was festooned in coral necklaces. Tweeds were more in her line.

We went in to dinner. Mary and I talked about horses. She came of a hunting family in the north of England, and had had her own pony from the age of three. She liked to have horses around, even though she couldn't hunt anymore; she missed that more than anything. Though, of course, dogs were better than nothing, she agreed. 'I should have been a veterinary surgeon,' she said with a laugh.

On the other side of me I could hear Chumly describing the latest radio innovations in great technical detail to Dr. Crawford. She seemed to be listening to him intently — but her eye flickered ever so faintly as it caught mine.

Dinner over, and back in the sitting-room, we arranged ourselves into a bridge four: Mary and I against Chumly and Helen. Mary had a fine card-sense, and played with unflustered reliability. Helen, on the other hand, had a certain verve and dash about her playing, and a gambler's recklessness in her occasional bouts of frantic over-calling. With nervous determination, Chumly consistently over-called. He was an inexperienced player. And I play a cautious, slow and thoroughly dull game. So now I obediently followed Mary's game, and on the side studied their play characteristics.

Presently the phone rang. The maid

came in with it in her hand, and plugged it into the wall. 'It's for you, Doctor,' she said, handing it to Dr. Fortescue.

'Excuse me,' she said. 'Hullo . . . Yes . . . ? Oh! It's you, dear. What is it . . . ? My poor child . . . but of course . . . No, it's no trouble; don't be silly . . . I'll just finish this bridge game and come down right away . . . Oh, they won't mind; Helen will understand.' She turned to us and put her hand over the mouthpiece. 'It's Nancy. She isn't feeling too good. She'd like me down there, I think.' She turned back to the phone. 'All right . . . If it's all the same to you, I'll come down after the rubber . . . Don't be silly, child . . . Yes, goodbye.' She put down the receiver. 'She's got a little panicky. I don't suppose it's anything at all; but you know what some women get like when it's a first pregnancy. And I do feel that at a time like this she ought not to be left much alone.' She was shuffling the cards as she spoke. 'As a matter of fact, I wanted her to come and stay with me — but she wouldn't. She said she'd rather be alone.'

'You're right. She ought not to be alone,' said Dr. Crawford as she flipped the cards round the table. 'But all the same, I don't think she ought to trail you out at this time of night; she ought to have more consideration.'

'Oh, well!' Dr. Fortescue shrugged tolerantly. And the game proceeded. But the rubber was a long one; and, contrary to our expectations, Helen and Chumly won. Mary leant back in her chair wearily with a wan, distressed smile.

'Mary, you're not going down to that child tonight,' said Dr. Crawford determinedly. 'It's insane. You're overtaxing your strength. I'm going to phone her up, and tell her I'm coming down instead.'

'No, you can't do that,' said Mary hurriedly. 'I said I'd go. I don't suppose it's anything. She won't keep me a minute. I shall take down some capsules. What I always take myself for those nervous digestive pains — and I'm sure that's all it is with her.'

'All the more reason,' Helen pursued her relentlessly, 'for you not to trail all that way out. Why can't Chumly take

190

them down for you? And then if it *is* anything, he can see to it. You'd be glad to do that, wouldn't you, Chumly?'

'Certainly. Of course.'

'There you are, then. It's absurd to argue further. Chumly will drive you home in his car. You give him the tablets, plus a message that you'll come down first thing in the morning, and that is that,' she arranged decisively.

Dr. Fortescue seemed suddenly too tired to argue. She crumpled and gave in with a sigh. Tenderly, Helen packed her into her coat and bade her goodnight.

When they had gone, she said apologetically, 'What a rotten evening this has been for you. You won't go yet, will you? Have a drink? What would you like to do?'

I glanced at my wristwatch. 'Would you like to run into Garrangarth? I think I have enough petrol; it isn't far, is it? Perhaps we could find a little fun there, even if it's only somewhere to dance.'

'I'd love to,' she said. 'You've hit my mood. I feel like *doing* something. I want to get away from it for a bit and do something a bit crazy. After all,' she added, half-reproachfully, 'it is my holiday.'

The village was blacked out as we drove through, but I noticed Chumly's car outside Mrs. Royd's house.

'Do you think he's got his eye on that little thing?' I asked. 'He jumped at the chance of going down there, didn't he?'

'Well, he's very young, and she's very pretty.'

'But do you think there's anything in it? Pre-Royd. I mean.'

'Good heavens, no!' She laughed. 'She was completely submerged in Royd, and would never have thought of looking at another man. She wasn't so madly in love with him — though she was once, I think — but he utterly dominated her. And as for Chumly, I should hope he was too much of a public schoolboy to even think of such a thing — while her husband was alive.'

'You have the most unpleasant way of knocking down all my carefully built-up suspects,' I grumbled. 'Get out of my car at once.'

She descended with dignity and walked through the stucco portals into the Garrangarth Grand Hotel. But Garrangarth evidently considered that twelve o'clock was late enough. The old-fashioned plush and gilt ballroom was empty — save for two couples, who rose and left as we came in, and half a dozen yawning waiters flapping their napkins over the empty tables. The female five-piece band tactlessly whined out, 'It's Time to Say Goodnight'.

★ ★ ★

Inspector Trevor called in to see me next morning. His rubicund face was glum. 'You haven't heard the news yet, have you? Thought I'd better come and tell you. Mrs. Royd is dead.'

'Dead?' I was incredulous. 'When? How? I don't understand. It wasn't — murder, was it?'

'No,' he reassured me. 'But suicide, I'm afraid. I think it was the maid who found her this morning. I don't know — '

'Suicide? That child! Good Lord,

Trevor, it isn't possible. How horrible! Have you any idea why?'

He shook his head. 'She was a nice little thing,' he said gloomily. 'I suppose it was the shock of all this business. 'The balance of her mind was disturbed' sort of thing.'

I snorted my contempt. 'She was as cool as a clam about it. I'm going down there right away; pass me my coat. Have you considered that my original guess may be right after all?'

'What was that?'

'That Mrs. Royd was the killer,' I called over my shoulder.

The little maid was crying when she opened the door to me. I went straight upstairs. The bedroom was the first facing the stairs. She lay in bed, her head turned sideways with her cheek nestling in the pillow, in a waxen sleep. I looked about me. No sign of disorder anywhere. The dainty feminine dressing-table was covered with numbers of little bottles and jars, but nothing appeared to be out of place. Her bedside table held a lamp, a jug of water and a glass, a tiny bookcase. I ran my hand under the pillow and bolster. Nothing. Gently shook the sheets about her shoulders. Looked under the bed, and turned back the edge of the rug. Nothing.

I pressed the bell for the girl. When she came, I told her to sit down. 'I understand that you found your mistress?'

She nodded speechlessly. I persuaded her to tell me about it. It appeared that she had come in as usual with the early morning tea at seven o'clock, but that Mrs. Royd seemed to be sleeping so soundly she hadn't the heart to wake her. She had come up again at eight with her breakfast and, unable to waken her by calling, had put down the tray and shaken her ... She'd gone a bit queer herself after that, but just as soon as she could she had gone downstairs and telephoned to Dr. Fortescue and asked her to come at once.

'Was the room just like this when you came in? You didn't notice a little bit of paper or anything like that lying about? You didn't throw anything away? No. By the way, what time did Dr. Chumly leave last night?'

'Dr. Chumly, sir? I didn't know he'd been here. I knew the mistress rang up Dr. Fortescue to ask her to come round, on account of how she was feeling rather poorly. But after that she said I could go to bed, as she'd let the doctor in when she came. And I must have gone right off to sleep, for I never heard no one come, sir.'

'How did your mistress seem in herself? Any different from usual?'

'Well, sir, I did notice she wasn't looking well — sort of upset and feverish. But she didn't seem unhappy, I don't think. I particularly noticed, when I was clearing away the supper things, how she was smiling to herself in a kind of way, and I was ever so glad, 'cos I thought it meant she was feeling better. And all the time, the poor thing . . . ' Tears filled her eyes.

'I daresay Dr. Royd had one of those little medicine chests that he kept his medical samples and suchlike in, didn't he?'

'Yes, sir, he did. It's downstairs in his

study. I'll show you.' She led me downstairs into a small room off the hall.

Dr. Fortescue and Helen were in the study. Dr. Fortescue had been crying, I observed. As I came in, Mary got to her feet and said gruffly that she must get back to the hospital to her patients. I suggested that, as she was here, it might be as well if she stayed for a bit, for she could probably help me a lot.

Helen whispered to me to let her go; she was horribly upset by this, and in no state to be questioned. But I had a job to do, and the sooner I got down to it the better for all concerned. I regretted that I had to worry them at such a time. I thought Dr. Fortescue would appreciate my position.

Of course, she did absolutely. Helen was being unreasonable, from the best of motives, for she was perfectly all right. This settled, I asked her how long Mrs. Royd had been dead when she examined the body.

'Not very long; perhaps half an hour or an hour, I'd say. *Rigor mortis* had not commenced. I tried — I did what I could

. . . But it was too late.' She ran her fingers through her hair.

'Have you any idea of the cause of death?'

'Impossible to be certain, but considering the outward appearance of the body, I conjecture that it was a narcotic. There'll have to be a post-mortem.'

'You don't think, then, that death could have occurred from natural causes?' I asked.

'Young girls in normal health with no organic disease are hardly likely to drop dead for no reason at all. Mrs. Royd was my patient, and I know that functionally and organically she was sound,' said Dr. Fortescue sharply.

'But she was not well yesterday, was she? Supposing — '

'Quite. Supposing I had done my duty and come down to see her last night, this might never have happened. That was what you were going to say, weren't you?' In that harsh voice.

'Mary, don't blame yourself!' said Dr. Crawford. 'You sent Dr. Chumly. That was all that was necessary. He's not a fool; he could quite well have diagnosed her if there was anything wrong with her.'

'Have either of you seen Dr. Chumly and heard his opinion yet? Does he know what has happened?' I asked.

Dr. Crawford said, 'No! I'd forgotten all about him. Listen, perhaps he did think there was something wrong with her, Mary, and prescribed something for her himself.'

Her face lightened at the thought, but settled again into misery as she shook her head. 'He wouldn't do that. I particularly told him to fetch me out if there was anything at all seriously wrong with her,' she said.

'All the same, it will help a lot to get hold of Chumly, wherever he is. Dr. Crawford, might I ask you to phone up the hospital for me and get hold of Chumly? Thank you so much. I want to find Royd's medicine-chest. Possibly — '

'There it is.' Dr. Fortescue pointed to a neat oak cabinet about four feet high. 'But I don't think you'll find it very helpful. So far as I could see, nothing had been touched. Well,' she went on defensively, in answer to my look of annoyance, 'I had to see if she had taken anything from there. If I had known what it was, there might perhaps have been a faint chance of saving her.'

I was running my eye over the shelves as she spoke. There were the usual antiseptics and appliances, a shelf full of common drugs, and two shelves crammed with samples and advertising produce. Nothing appeared to have been disturbed. But, of course, Dr. Fortescue might have unintentionally rearranged things during her own search, and most of the samples were unopened.

'Where could she have got hold of anything?' I puzzled. 'Is it possible that she could have taken something from the hospital dispensary?'

'Hardly. There is almost always someone there. But even if she did slip by with anything, I should have thought they would notice when they checked through the supplies at the end of the day. Still, it is just a possibility. We have to take great precautions in regard to that, you see, on account of the patients. So many of them have suicidal tendencies ... I can't imagine what would happen to the hospital if we ever lost a patient through that sort of criminal carelessness,' she finished with a shiver.

'You know, Dr. Fortescue, I was more than surprised when I heard the news this morning. I should never have thought Mrs. Royd was a suicidal type, or in a suicidal frame of mind. I would like to have your professional opinion on that. Were you equally surprised?'

Dr. Fortescue fidgeted nervously with her coral necklace. 'Yes and no. I'm afraid I can't be precise. I do know it was a terrific shock to me, I did not want to believe it. And yet — will you think me foolish if I say that it was as if I suddenly realised that I had had a premonition of a pending disaster, and the disaster itself made me retrospectively conscious of the premonition?' She gave a nervous laugh. 'For the rest, strictly speaking, there are no suicidal types. When certain hereditary and environmental aspects coincide or occur sequentially, they produce — or are liable to produce — certain morbid characteristics that have been casually designated as 'typically' suicidal. I agree with you, however, that Nancy Royd did not exhibit these characteristics. As to whether she was in a suicidal frame of mind — I think she was. I didn't realise it at the time. But I know that for so placid — or I should say, self-contained — a person, she was in a very hysterical condition. It didn't worry me unduly, because women in her condition often become somewhat excited or depressed in the early stages of pregnancy, and in her case this was not surprising.'

'You mean, on account of losing her husband in such shocking circumstances? By the way, how far advanced was the pregnancy?' I asked.

'About two and a half months, I gather. No, her husband's death would not account for her hysterical attitude. I think I ought to tell you, Mr. Chaos, that she did not want the child. She asked — she wanted me to procure her an abortion.'

'When was this?'

'On the Monday morning. The day Dr.

Royd was murdered.'

'I see. Please tell me about it.'

She brushed her hand wearily over her forehead. 'Yes. Naturally, I told her I could do no such thing. I explained to her that it is a criminal offence. I reasoned with her. I thought at first she was frightened of bearing a child, and I explained that there was nothing to fear, particularly as both she and her husband were fine, healthy specimens. It was not that. She admitted after a while that it was his child that she did not wish to have. And, she said, nothing on earth would induce her to bear it, she would kill herself sooner. But that, I felt — and still feel — was said more to try to frighten me into giving in to her than with any real intention of self-destruction. I gather that she had tried to bring on a miscarriage herself with drugs, but fortunately was too healthy. Women, I told her, often feel a kind of revulsion early in pregnancy; it is merely a physiological upheaval, and automatically adjusts itself in time.

'Then she — she burst into tears,' continued Dr. Fortescue, in a deliberately dry voice, 'and said it wasn't that at all. 'Don't you understand,' she cried to me, 'that I hate him! Hate and loathe and detest him with all my heart and soul,' she went on vehemently. 'I would rather die than bear a child of his . . . than perpetuate that mind. You don't know, Mary, what he's like. On the surface he is all right, a handsome albeit domineering man. Underneath, Maurice is a devil — the cruellest, most vicious kind of devil imaginable . . . with ideas in his head to make your blood run cold.'

'She saw that I thought she was exaggerating, and she offered to provide me with a few examples . . . Mr. Chaos, I am an elderly woman who has spent the greater part of her life in handling abnormality — I wouldn't say I was particularly shockable. But I assure you that what that poor child told me made me feel cold and sick.' She shuddered now at the recollection. 'Again, the child begged me to help her. I tried to make her see that such characteristics were not hereditary; and finally that she could leave him — if not now, then as soon as the child was born. However, she wouldn't listen. She went away almost at once.'

'She never approached you again on the subject?'

Dr. Fortescue shook her head. She looked exhausted.

'Did you think she had given up the idea?'

She stared out of the window. 'To be honest, I didn't want to know. It was her business. I had washed my hands of it — just like Pilate,' she added bitterly. 'I don't approve of abortion, and so I wouldn't help her, poor baby. But if someone else wanted to take the responsibility, I was not going to interfere. And then, too, I did quite honestly think that now her husband was dead, she would not feel so strongly against the baby ... ' She laughed shortly. 'It seems I was wrong, however.'

There was a rap on the door and Chumly poked his head round. 'Shall I come in? Dr. Crawford said you wanted me. I met her just going into the hospital, and she told me the shocking news and that Mr. Chaos wanted to see me.' He turned to Dr. Fortescue. 'She asked me to tell you, Doctor, that she was taking over your patients for the time being.'

'How sweet she is,' said Dr. Fortescue gratefully.

'Then I won't keep you any longer,' I said. 'I've been very hard on you already. Perhaps you could rest for a bit.'

When she had gone, I turned to Chumly and asked him to tell me just what had transpired after he had left Helen's the night before.

He had driven Dr. Fortescue home, and she had given him the phial of capsules, which he had taken down to Mrs. Royd. He had stayed there a few minutes chatting to her in a friendly way, and then had left as it was already getting late.

'How did she seem in herself then?'

'She seemed all right. A bit pale and excitable, I thought, but she said the pain was better. I asked if she would like me to examine her. And she laughed and said no, she was perfectly all right, she had just been making a fuss about nothing. I saw no reason not to believe her. I thought possibly she was really feeling lonely, and that was the real reason why she wished to see Dr. Fortescue. So I stayed for a while to keep her company.'

'Did she seem at all depressed?'

'No. Rather the contrary, I thought. Buoyant and excited. Very much as if she had just made an important decision and it was a great weight off her mind.'

'I see. And what about the capsules? Did you give them to her? Do you know whether she took them?'

'Yes, I gave them to her. She didn't want to take them at first, said she was better now. But I persuaded her to, finally.'

'Why?'

'Why what? Oh, it was quite a harmless preparation, and I thought it might do her good. Calm her down a little for the night . . . an anodyne, you know.'

'What happened to the phial? Have you any idea?' I asked.

'Eh? The phial?' He looked blank. 'I took it away with me.'

'What did you want to do that for?'

'The psychological factor, y'see. I tipped them out for her to take, and left them on the table by her bed. If I had merely left the tube, she might not have bothered to open it and tip out the capsules. But if they lie unwrapped and exposed to one's very eyes, it's almost impossible to resist the temptation not to waste them.'

'So you carried off the tube? What did you do with it?'

'I've no idea. Does it matter? It was just the ordinary phial these proprietary brands are always put up in.'

'It does matter,' I said grimly. 'I'd be obliged if you would find it for me. So far as we *know*, Dr. Chumly, those capsules were the last thing she took.'

The blood rushed away from his cheeks, leaving his skin a pasty green. 'You — you don't think — ' he stammered.

'I don't think anything,' I said. 'It is an obvious piece of routine work to examine that phial . . . Tell me, as a psychiatrist, why do you suppose Mrs. Royd took her life? She was young, healthy and pretty.

Do you think she was very cut up about her husband's death?'

'Frankly, I don't know . . . ' Suddenly he snapped his fingers. 'Have you considered that she may have been the person you were looking for? That it might be Mrs. Royd who killed the doctor?'

'That's very interesting,' I said. 'But do you think Mrs. Royd did in fact feel emotions of hate enough to murder?'

'So far as I know, she didn't; but my knowledge of her was extremely limited, after all.' He was a little huffy.

'But Dr. Royd knew her pretty well, I suppose, and was a man of some experience. Wouldn't he have known if she felt like that? Been on his guard? Besides, could she have slipped past Miss Brace twice without her noticing?'

'Somebody had to,' he reminded me.

'Yes, but any of the hospital people could get by without comment, whereas Mrs. Royd — '

'Yes, I see what you mean. Still, I do think it is worth looking into.'

'Who do you suppose will do the post-mortem?'

'Dr. Fortescue, I expect. Unless she feels too upset about it. I suppose we'll have one of the chaps from Garrangarth County Hospital over to analyse the doings.'

'Yes. Well, I expect that both inquests will be held together. It will save having to summon two lots of jurymen.'

His mouth opened. 'The inquest!' he said. 'I'd quite forgotten the inquest . . . '

# 13

'You Killed Her, Damn your Eyes!'

After Chumly left, I sat down at Royd's desk and went through his papers. Everything seemed in order. His cheque-stubs were discretion itself. Except for a few familiar trade-names, they were almost all of them made out to 'Self' or for cash.

At the back of a narrow stationery drawer, my groping fingers encountered and brought to light a little red leather-bound diary. I flicked over the leaves. Most of the dates were left blank; there was just an occasional jotting here and there . . .

*May 12th, C, 7.30; May 15th, C, 10; May 19th, C, 9.* And so on. Then in June there was, amongst numbers similar to the above: *June 25th, Saw C 50 . . . July 17th, Saw C 25 . . .* And in August there was *Saw C 100*; and later in the month,

*See McI re Pratt* . . . And more of the numbered dates marked *C* . . . I slipped it into my pocket.

When I had cleared up in the study, I went to the phone and rang Helen to ask her if she would lunch with me. She agreed to meet me at The Three Crows at one.

She was late, and came in looking pale, her face stiff and set.

'I was nearly unable to come,' she announced, grimly. 'Mary . . . I didn't like to leave her. She is so distraught over all this. She feels she is responsible for it. It's because she's ill herself, of course . . . ' She rested her forehead wearily in the palm of her hand. 'Oh, Jacob, I feel so wretched. Isn't it all a ghastly business?'

I ordered a couple of drinks, wondering whether she knew she had called me by my first name.

'Drink up,' I ordered. 'You're letting it get out of proportion yourself, you know. Now, we're not even going to mention it until we've had our meal.'

Afterwards, her tense face relaxed and

its normal colour returned. I started the ball rolling with recounting to her what Dr. Fortescue, Dr. Chumly and the maid had told me earlier.

She listened intently until I was finished.

'About this abortion . . . ' she said. 'Now I can tell you that that was Nancy's real reason for coming to see me yesterday. She wanted me to do it for her. Oh, she begged and implored . . . was altogether hysterical. I told her I couldn't . . . I mean, if there had been some justification — hereditary disease, a case of rape, for instance . . . I don't feel so rigid about it as Mary does. I believe that there are occasions when it is legitimate — but I did not think that this happened to be one of them. Of course, that was when she told me about Mary. She pretended that the only reason Mary wouldn't undertake it for her was because she was not well herself. I knew very well that was not the truth, but she was getting a little difficult to handle . . . And then you sent up your name, and I let you come up, even though we were both so on edge, because I thought the presence of a third person might have a calming and restraining influence. The rest, you know.'

'That did puzzle me somewhat,' I admitted. 'I wish you had told me the truth at the time; it would have made it so much easier for me.'

'How could I? You know it is not professional etiquette.'

'Professional etiquette be — ed!' I said sweetly. 'And, talking of not telling things, I didn't tell you what Nancy told Dr. Fortescue about her husband, did I?'

I proceeded to do so. 'Dr. Fortescue couldn't or wouldn't repeat what Nancy Royd had told her, but she was obviously horrified by it. And, as she said, she is a woman of some experience.'

Helen looked amused. 'I should be rather chary of accepting that just at its face value. Even if true, it might not have been so dire as Dr. Fortescue gave you to understand. She is experienced professionally, but she is not exactly what I would call a woman of the world; she still retains a childlike old-fashioned belief in the innate goodness of human nature.

But, anyway, I think there are quite good grounds for discounting it altogether. After all, Nancy had to put up some excuse to Dr. Fortescue. I believe she used the one she calculated as most likely to touch Mary's tender heart. She put up quite a different one for me, you see. And I don't see why, on the face of it, one should be any truer than the other.'

'Could be something in that,' I agreed. 'Have you any idea of her real reason for wanting an abortion? No? Do you think she killed herself because of it, because she couldn't procure herself one?'

Again she shook her head blankly.

'I wish to God she'd had the forethought to leave a note,' I grumbled. 'Not a word of farewell or apology . . . Not even a message to the coroner. Doesn't that seem most unnatural to you?'

'It isn't usual, perhaps,' she conceded, 'but quite often I have found that when a person commits suicide utterly impulsively, he leaves no hint of anything behind . . . Just doesn't care or bother. And then, too, often when they're just faking and just want to attract attention or frighten someone, they don't bother to go to all the trouble of writing a farewell letter.'

'Mmm, maybe. But that wasn't our Nancy, was it? Or do you think it was in the nature of an accident, and that she never really intended to kill herself at all? It will bear looking into. For the other, I don't much care for the theory of 'impulse' — it doesn't seem to *me* to follow at all. It wasn't an impulsive sort of suicide, it was slow.'

'It is true that these impulsive types generally dive out of a window, or make a clean sweep with a razor,' she said.

'How did she do it, I'd like to know. She was so dashed careful not to leave any clues for me . . . Hullo, I wonder if that is one of those true words spoken in jest. Was that why she left no trace of what the stuff was, or how she took it?' I pondered.

'But why should she want to make a mystery of it?'

I didn't know the answer to that one. 'I hope the post-mortem will explain quite a lot,' I said. 'Oh, Lord, look at the time. I must go and put my nose back to the grindstone.' I paid the bill, and together we strolled down the road towards Royd's house. It was clouding up heavily, big, rolling nimbus clouds sweeping in from the north-west. I sniffed the pungent air.

'It's going to rain,' I said, as I opened the gate.

'Yes. I must get back. Well, thank you very much for the luncheon, Mr. Chaos. I enjoyed — '

'You called me Jacob before lunch,' I remarked.

'Did I? Well, I was in a bit of a state, you know' she said, half-apologetically.

'Need we be so ceremonious?' I pleaded. 'Mayn't I call you Helen?'

'Might that not look a little — ' She hesitated.

'Unprofessional? Well, off-duty, at least. That wouldn't matter, would it?'

She twinkled at me. 'Very well, Jacob,' she said with mock-meekness. 'Thank you very much for the luncheon, Jacob. And now I must — oh!' She broke off as the rain descended in a cloudburst.

I dragged her into the porch. 'You'd better come in till this is over . . . Hullo, the door is open. Come on in. Where is the girl? Done a bunk, do you suppose? I'd better have a look for her.'

The kitchen was empty but disordered. Pots and pans stood on the unlit stove. Dirty utensils were piled in the sink. A kitchen chair stood in the middle of the room, as if someone had hurriedly pushed it back from the table as they rose to their feet.

'Look!' I said. 'Wherever she went, she went just as she was. Didn't even stop to put on a coat. There it is hanging behind the door. But she remembered to turn off the stove. The haste might imply that it was urgent. Leaving the door open, and not bothering about a coat in this weather, suggests that she may not have gone far, or that she may have expected to return in a few minutes.'

'Of course, she might be lying in one of the other rooms in a dead faint all this while,' suggested Helen, blandly.

'We will go and see. Your honour, Watson,' I said, holding the door.

No results downstairs; we proceeded upstairs. At the head of the stairs I halted her. A sound had reached my ears. A faint but unmistakable moaning. It came from Mrs. Royd's room. I pushed Helen gently to one side, and quietly turned the handle. A man knelt by the bed, his torso sprawling across the dead woman, his hands blindly and restlessly stroking her hair and face. And all the while he moaned . . .

Helen tiptoed in after me. 'Christie!' she exclaimed, and clapped her hand over her mouth.

At the sound of her voice the man turned round defensively. And with a start of surprise I recognised the stalwart young man of the tree incident.

Helen said: 'Mr. Christie, what are you doing here?'

He gazed at her blankly. 'She's dead,' he muttered, brokenly. 'I don't understand . . . Why should she be dead . . . ?'

'She's dead because she killed herself,' I said suddenly.

'What's that you say? Killed herself? Who are you? That's what they told me up there: that she killed herself. But it isn't true.' His voice rose sharply shrill. 'It's a damned dirty lie . . . She never killed herself.' He sprang to his feet. 'I know . . . she was killed.'

'Now, Mr. Christie, calm yourself. It — ' Helen stepped forward.

His head lowered like a bull's, he pointed a shaking finger at her. 'You killed her, you killed her, damn your eyes!' he screamed dementedly. 'I'll kill you for that, God damn your soul to hell!' He started towards her, his chest heaving tremendously, and suddenly stopped in his tracks with a stricken expression on his face. His breath whined in his throat. He clutched at his chest with convulsive hands, and his eyes were terrified.

Again Helen went towards him. And again he stopped her.

'Don't touch me, don't touch me . . . damn you . . . ' he panted hoarsely, and began staggering about the room, waving his arms about. 'Oh God, oh God,' he panted, 'I can't stand this . . . ' He lurched over to the closed window and struck at the pane with a frantic gesture. His fist went through the glass with the brief noise of aerial machine-gun fire, letting in a gust of rain-chilled air. He leant against the window-frame and sucked in the air noisily.

'This won't do, Mr. Christie,' said Helen gently. 'Look what you've done to your hand.'

He stared down at his hand, from which the blood was dropping in great purple gouts on to the beige carpet.

'You'd better let me fix it for you,' she went on firmly. 'Come downstairs into the study. I've got some things down there, bandages and antiseptic . . . ' With a hand on his elbow, she steered him towards the door.

I followed them slowly into the study. She had got him sitting on the couch, and was bathing his hand in a kidney bowl. The hand was badly cut, but she strapped it up neatly with her deft, capable fingers. His spasm, or whatever it was, had passed now, but he looked grey and pinched beneath his ruddy tan.

When she had tied the final bandage, Helen said, 'Lie down here quietly for a bit and rest. That was a nasty cut.'

Obediently, he leant back against the arm and swung up his legs. He closed his eyes.

The rain had stopped now and the sun had come out again. Helen walked over to the window and leant pensively against the breast-high sill. I scribbled on a scrap of paper and passed it across to her.

She read, *What is it all about and where do we go from here?* and smiled. She found a pencil stub in her jacket pocket, and bent over the sill. She rolled the answer into a pellet and flicked it across to me. It read: *I mean to try and find out. May I? He's my patient and it is as much in his interests as in yours that I want to clear it up.* I nodded. She signalled to me to get back out of his field of vision . . .

I sat down in a chair near the door, and behind the head of the couch. Helen cleared her throat and said in her low, kind voice, 'Mr. Christie, what are you thinking about as you lie there?'

'I'm trying not to think about anything, Doctor,' he said in an empty, bitter sort of voice. 'I feel quite extraordinarily ill.'

'I expect you do. The loss of blood, for one thing, and then all that excitement before that, and earlier still the shock of — '

'Oh, don't, please.' He threw his forearm across his eyes.

'Why do you want to run away from it? It will be much easier for you if you bring it out and face it. You know that,' she urged. 'Why were you so frightened to learn that Mrs. Royd was dead?'

He drew in his breath with a sob, but refused to answer.

'Consider what is best for yourself, Mr. Christie. It may be painful now, but it will be a great load off your mind later. What loyalty do you owe to Mrs. Royd? Why must you suffer for her? She is dead. You are alive.'

'Nothing will induce me to discuss it with you,' he said stiffly through his clenched teeth.

Helen sighed and made a face at me. There was a pause. I looked at her as she stood there, her nut-brown hair touched to fiery red where the sunbeams met it.

As if conscious of my eyes, she put up her hand to her curls to smooth them. The immense topaz she wore on her finger winked in the sun and dazzled me. She kept her hand there, and so I quietly moved the chair an inch or two out of the line of refracted light.

She was talking to Christie. 'Look at me,' she commanded. 'Now, seriously, don't you think it absurd to tense yourself up like this against your own doctor? What is there that you can't safely tell me? Believe me, it's actually dangerous . . . ' Her voice went on: a smooth, colourless flow.

He stared at her but made no response. 'No, don't close your eyes. I'll tell you when to do that. You're feeling sleepy, aren't you? Naturally . . . Sleep is what you need . . . Plenty of soothing sleep . . . You can close your eyes now if you like. But you won't go right off to sleep. You can still hear me talk, can't you? That's right. Because I want you to answer some questions for me. Are you well relaxed . . . ? Good. You are beginning to feel much better . . . Who told you that Mrs. Royd was dead? Oh, the porter? What did you do then? Tell me in your own words. See if you can remember every little thing. Go back in your mind now to when the porter told you . . . What happened then? What did you think? What did you do? What did you say?'

He began talking in a rapid, rather dreamy monotone. 'I felt as if someone had kicked me where it would hurt most, when Smith told me. And he looked at me in that horrid sly way and said, 'Oh, yes, she is. And what's more, she killed herself.' I wanted to be sick or faint or smash something . . . Then I thought the best thing would be to go and see what had happened. Of course, I knew I ought not to go to the house, that it was foolhardy in any case; but I couldn't help myself. I tumbled down the drive and ran all the way to the house. I suppose I must have rung the bell, because a maid answered the door. I noticed that she had been crying, and it was then, I think, that I began to believe that something awful had occurred. I was afraid.

'The maid asked me what I wanted. She was looking at me queerly, and I suppose I did look a bit off. I couldn't think what I ought to say; I just panted at her and rolled my eyes. She gave a cry and asked me if I had come from home, I don't know why she thought that. I misunderstood her, thought she said *the* home, and nodded. Then she said, 'Is something wrong? Has there been an accident? Do they want me? Ooh, is it Lil or Mum? I'd best go right away,' and she scuttled away down the passage and left me there at the open door. I thought she might remember and mean to come back that way to shut it, so I slipped in quickly and went upstairs . . .

'I found her room and went in. I saw her lying there . . . dead,' he pronounced, his voice jarring like a needle jerking in the groove of a disc. 'So I called to her . . . But she wasn't there . . . She would have answered me if she had been. She was so kind . . . always so kind . . . ' The words grated to silence.

Helen said, 'What relation was Mrs. Royd to you?'

In that dreamy, almost absent-minded voice, he said, 'Nancy was my mistress. I loved her . . . '

Helen looked at me sideways. 'Why were you so angry when I said she had killed herself, Mr. Christie?' she queried.

'I knew it was a lie . . . I knew she hadn't killed herself . . . I knew she wouldn't kill herself,' said Christie. 'I might have believed it if she had killed herself *before* Royd's death, but after, no . . . '

'You mean, she hated Royd?' Helen suggested.

'I don't know,' he said vaguely. 'She may have hated him. I know she was afraid of him.'

Helen was about to speak again, but I held up my hand to stop her. I didn't want him to be sidetracked here; it was too important. I said, as discreetly as possible, 'What makes you so certain that Mrs. Royd did not kill herself?'

'There wasn't any reason for her to, now that *he* was dead.'

'Why should she have killed herself because her husband was alive?'

'I said she might have done. I would have believed it if she had then. She might have done because she was afraid. She was going to have a child, you see, and she was afraid he would find out. She didn't know what he would do if he found out it was not his child.'

'Was it yours?'

'Yes . . . '

'I see. So you think she might have committed suicide rather than face her husband if he found out? But that once that obstacle was removed — in the shape of his murder — she would have nothing more to fear? Is that right?' I couldn't look at Helen.

'I think so . . . I am a little confused . . . ' His voice trailed off.

'In effect, you believe Nancy Royd was murdered?' I said.

He jerked himself higher on the couch. 'Yes, yes. That's clear enough, isn't it? Someone killed my Nancy, I know it.'

'Have you any idea who — ?' I began, but at that moment he started to shake all over as if afflicted with a rigor . . .

Helen stepped forward swiftly and

shook her head at me.

'That's enough.' she said firmly. She took Mr. Christie's hand in hers, and sat on the edge of the couch beside him. 'It's all right, Mr. Christie. Relax. Loosen up and let yourself go limp . . . Can you feel your heels pressing into the couch . . . ? Hips . . . Spine . . . You're weighing down heavily; that's right . . . Tummy relaxed? Slow, deep, even breaths . . . Arms, hands, fingers . . . that's the way . . . Neck, jaw, tongue . . . eyes . . . heavy as lead . . . Ah, now you're feeling much better . . . much better . . . You are sleeping as deeply and contentedly as a baby . . . Lovely deep sleep . . . And when you wake up, you will feel quite well . . . '

I stood beside Helen, and watched him as he slept. He was as lovely as Endymion, with his ruddy, almost beardless, face; and the long dark lashes lying on his cheeks and making him look childlike and defenceless. His limbs were well shaped and neatly jointed, his shoulders powerful and muscular. I could imagine what a lovely pair he and Nancy must have made: he so dark and strong, she so small and fair. Easy to understand, what they had seen in one another. And then I remembered that Nancy was dead and would never delight anyone on this earth again, and that Christie was ill, and unstable mentally. I stared at the handsome young thing incredulously. *Like an elm-tree*, came the thought . . . they all resembled elms in that they might appear beautiful and sound on the outside and yet be utterly rotten within . . . rotten and ready to crash to the ground without any further warning; and if you were in the way, so much the worse for you . . .

Helen said, 'It's time to wake up, Mr. Christie. You have had a beautiful sleep and are feeling much better now. Wake up!'

The dark lashes flicked back with the precision of a mechanical doll's. He yawned, then smiled at Helen amiably. My legs came within his field of vision, and his eyes travelled up curiously to my head, then stared about him at his unfamiliar surroundings. I saw comprehension dawn like a sunrise, and then memory return like a moonless night. His face crumpled in alarm.

'There, there!' said Helen, soothingly. 'You've forgotten that you told us all about it before you went to sleep. It's all right. There is nothing to fear. Listen to me.' She began to recapitulate what he had told us earlier. He listened attentively, though his face was darkly flushed. I didn't need to hear all that again, so I stepped out to see if the maid had returned.

She was standing at the sink, washing up. She let out a scream when she saw me. 'Oh! Sir, wherever did you come from?' she gasped. I told her. She was horrified. 'It was that young man,' she said. 'I've been that upset all day,' she added, by way of excuse, 'that I suppose I was ready to believe the worst about anything. Didn't 'arf feel a fool when I got 'ome, though . . . And oh, sir, Mum says she don't 'arf dislike the idea of me sleeping here alone with 'er tonight.' She jerked an expressive thumb upwards. I reassured her that she could go home and spend the night with Mum, and I would arrange for someone to look after things here. She looked relieved.

'You have never seen this young man before today, then?'

She shook her head emphatically. 'I'd remember if I 'ad, sir. Ever so good-looking, isn't 'e?' She opened the back door and leant out to place a bundle of rubbish, neatly wrapped in a piece of newspaper, in the dustbin. I saw it was crammed with papers. I commented on the fact pretty sharply.

'It's only a lot of old papers, sir — gardening catalogues and such that were always cluttering up the sitting-room. I didn't think it would matter throwing 'em out now.'

I intimated that the sooner she rescued them from the bin the better. 'Fancy throwing out paper nowadays!' I said disgustedly, sorting them into piles as I spoke. Catalogues, order-sheets, illustrated gardening papers, odd notes . . . There didn't seem to be anything of importance; maybe I was too hopeful and had made a fuss about nothing. And then, at the bottom of the pile, wedged in between some old weeklies, was Carter's Seedbook, a National Blue Book and a linen-bound gardener's journal . . . Inside, the pages were covered with hieroglyphics, indecipherable scrawls. I frowned over them . . . Of course, how stupid of me! I had done shorthand as a lad, and I still retained faint recollections of the outlines. (Had Nancy Royd been a secretary before her marriage?) Was this going to be of any use to me, or was it only about gardening? Speed had probably been the chief consideration, of course, but it did seem to me that there was something rather secretive about putting one's diary into cipher — even such a common one as this.

Laboriously, I translated the signs into sounds. Perhaps I just happened to strike lucky, but I saw enough to make me close the book and cram it into the poacher's pocket in my tweed jacket.

Helen came in. 'I'm going back to the hospital now with Mr. Christie, if that's all right by you.'

'Just a minute.' I turned to Christie and added in a low voice, 'You don't know who I am, do you?' I told him. 'If Mrs. Royd was murdered, I must find out who did it. I suppose you want her murderer to be brought to justice, don't you? But — the only reason we have to suppose that she was murdered rests on your evidence. Therefore, I ask you to substantiate your claims in some way. I can't very well accept this just on your word of mouth alone. Excuse me for saying this, but the whole thing may be fantasy. Will you give me some proof?'

He smiled a trifle grimly. 'Unless I'm a good deal crazier than I think I am, it did happen. Proof, what proof can I give you?'

'A letter, perhaps,' I suggested.

'She made me swear that I'd burn all her letters as soon as I'd read them. But I didn't.' He laughed mirthlessly. 'Perhaps it's just as well, eh?'

I suggested that I go up to the hospital with him there and then to collect them.

Afterwards Helen made me tea in her consulting-room. It had been an exhausting and astonishing afternoon.

'So Nancy was murdered,' she said. 'It

seems absolutely incredible to me. Why should anyone wish to murder that child?'

'That is what we shall have to find out.'

'Yes. Do you realise that if Christie's story is true, I was right when I said that she lied both to Mary and myself about her reason for wanting an abortion? Funny, that!' Helen poured some milk into the cups.

'I feel badly about this, Helen. I feel rather responsible. I should have foreseen the danger and been able to protect her.'

'How could you? Don't be absurd.'

'That's my job, Helen. I probably precipitated the whole thing. Maybe, the killer thought I was getting too hot. Or Nancy Royd knew too much. Be that as it may, if I had not been on the scene it might never have happened. That is the trouble with this delicate game: in trying to arrest the criminal, we often force him into a position from whence he can only escape — so he thinks — by covering his tracks with further crimes. If we didn't try to bring him to justice, maybe only one life would be lost, as it is the innocents who — No, that's nonsense,' I corrected myself. 'They would become bolder than ever that way.'

Helen looked white. 'Are you trying to tell me that you believe this is a follow-on from Royd's murder? That the same person is responsible for both?'

'Just that,' I said.

'But what makes you think so? I thought that criminals always committed the same sort of crime. But these crimes seem to me to be just about as different as they could be.'

I smiled wearily. 'The symptoms may differ, my dear, but the disease is the same. The criminal has made the one slip that all good criminals are supposed to make. I suppose I must be grateful to Nancy Royd for that. If she had not been sacrificed, I might never have solved the first murder. Now I know — what I wanted to know.'

Helen looked at me gravely. 'What was the slip?'

'Can't you guess?' I teased. 'What about the little grey cells, my friend?

She frowned. 'Don't joke, please, Jacob. What have you learnt?'

'I have learnt that the murder of Dr. Maurice Royd was premeditated,' I said soberly.

# 14

## 'He Was Trying to Blackmail Me'

Dr. McIvor stopped me in the passage.

'This is a terrible affair,' he said, gripping my arm. 'I am inexpressibly shocked. But we can't discuss it here. Please come into my room.' Once inside, he continued: 'Have you any idea why that poor little soul should have done such a thing? Was it grief, or — ?' He gazed at me hopefully.

'Or guilt, you wonder.' I supplied the word he was too timorous to use. 'I don't think it was either.'

'Fear, then . . . ? Or could it have been accident?' His tired face lit up at the thought. He was looking, I thought, rather more ill than before.

''Fraid not, Doctor. I ought not to tell you this before I have definite proof. But, as the Head of the hospital, it's perhaps right that you should know that — I have reason to believe Mrs. Royd was murdered.'

'Murdered,' he repeated, dully, wearily rubbing his eyes.

'It doesn't surprise you,' I commented.

'I rather expected that it wasn't going to end there. Poor little thing! Knew too much, I suppose. Who's going to be next?' He looked at me ironically. 'But that's your job, Mr. Chaos. You are here to protect us and bring the murderer to justice . . . I don't envy you your task.'

'It would be made a lot easier if people who have nothing to hide wouldn't take it into their heads that frankness is a sign of guilt. Just because their guilty act happens to coincide with the time of the murder, they fudge up nonsensical excuses that naturally arouse the worst suspicions in me. In consequence, I go haring off, wasting time and energy, all to no purpose.' I snorted.

He smiled. 'All right, I'll come clean. That's the expression, isn't it? What is it you want to know?'

'Just what is all the mystery about your Headship? What was it that Royd had discovered against you?'

'It happened when I'd been here about two years,' he said abruptly. 'I was a very ambitious young man, with big plans for a tremendous future. I was newly married, too. Harley Street within a stone's throw, and my own clinic just around the corner. And then a patient of mine kicked the bucket: he committed suicide. Of course, I was to blame: I should have foreseen it, and either got rid of him or removed temptation from him by seeing that he had a special nurse to remain with him constantly day and night. That put me in a nasty spot. At the least, it would mean that I would have to resign immediately. But I couldn't afford to leave just then. I hadn't saved a bean: every penny had gone on settling debts and straightening out my tangled affairs. Then, too, it would be bad for the hospital's reputation. Coroners make heavy weather over that sort of thing, with censures and so on.

'He was an elderly man with pronounced melancholia. He was not in good health; a sedentary life and a dicky heart. He'd been here two or three weeks, and I don't know to this day whether he had been able to secrete the medication somewhere in his room or on his person all that time, or whether he was able to procure some locally by bribery. Either way, he had swallowed enough luminal to kill him several times over with his rotten heart . . . No one knew anything about it. I was sure of that. The floor nurse, who had notified me, knew of his death — no more. She had not remarked on the little bottle by his bed. I felt safe enough . . . '

He was staring over my shoulder into the past. 'I made up my mind. I put the bottle in my pocket. I wrote on the certificate that death was due to heart disease, and signed it with a steady hand. That was that.'

'Was it not brought to light?'

He smiled. 'Of course it was! I'd been overconfident, you see. The little nurse *had* noticed the empty bottle of luminal, but had refrained from mentioning it out of modesty and discretion. But she kept an eye on me. And then one day, months after the man had been decently buried, I was hauling her over the coals for something when she stopped me. She told me what she suspected. 'You have no proof,' I said. 'No,' she replied, 'but it would make a very peculiar story and would require investigation. An exhumation order could raise a stink that nothing could quench.' I asked her why she hadn't taken her suspicions direct to the fountainhead. Then she began some sickening rigmarole . . . Ugh! In short, she seemed to fancy herself in love with me, and the price of her silence was — an affair with me. She was a nymphomaniac, of course. At the time I did not realise that she hoped for further blackmail from it — ultimately, that my wife would divorce me and I would be forced to marry her.' He laughed mirthlessly. 'She was altogether too ambitious, that lady. But I was far too much in love with my wife to consider such a loathsome project. I said, 'Publish and be damned!' '

'Did she?'

He nodded. 'She told the chief, and he forwarded her accusation to the Committee. I was had up for a private inquiry. However, they were afraid of a scandal. It was to our mutual advantage, then, to hush up the whole affair. And from then on, too, we practised a kind of mutual blackmail. I knew too much to be dismissed; they knew too much to raise me to a responsible post.' He laughed. 'So, you see, I had ruined my career just the same . . . '

I was sorry for this man who had smashed his future with one careless, frightened gesture . . . I said thoughtfully, 'By the way, what did Dr. Royd say to you when he spoke to you about Pratt last August?'

He ran his tongue over his pale lips. 'This is all off the record, isn't it? It was fundamentally the same thing over again. Miss Pratt was my patient. She managed the almost impossible by sneaking into the dispensary, stealing a lethal dose of a drug, and slipping out unobserved.

'We buy most of our drugs ready-made-up. Then, before they are administered to the patients, all pills or tablets are crushed into powder. A nurse tips them onto the patient's tongue herself. This prevents them from secreting pills under their tongues or in their cheeks instead of swallowing them, and so gradually accumulating enough to harm themselves with. All medicine is always taken in the presence of a nurse, otherwise they might throw it down the sink.

'Once in the dispensary, it was easy for her to remove a bottle of aspirin from the shelves.' His face was pallid with sweat and his voice shook.

'I'm begging you to believe,' he said, earnestly, 'that this time I did what I did from no selfish motive. It was simply and solely to safeguard the good name of the hospital. If I had been thinking of myself this time, I would never have been such an idiot. The first thing I did after attending to the woman was to quietly replace the missing drug from my private stock.

'Anyway, Royd found out about it. So that was the real reason he was trying to blackmail me. He hadn't any proof, of course, save that of the replaced drug. I clung like mad to my knowledge that he had no real evidence. Would he dare to ask for an exhumation order on such slender grounds?' He shook his head contemptuously. 'He didn't give a damn for scandal, but he would have hated making a fool of himself. So long as I did not let him see that I was scared, I was safe. Of course, as you suggested, I needed to be careful that he didn't fake up something against me. But I watched my step there . . . Well, I guess you've got the lot now.'

Did he realise, I wondered, that he had by no means cleared himself? Suppose Royd had fudged up something else, or had threatened to inform the Committee of his suspicions? There was motive there to invite his murder.

I sighed and rose to go. 'You won't forget those papers, will you?' I reminded him.

I carried away with me the memory of his anxious haunted eyes.

On my way out of the hospital I stopped off at the library to look for a book. Apparently the elegant Mrs. Harrison was the librarian. 'And what can I do for you, sir?'

'I thought you might have a 'Pitman's Shorthand' I could borrow.'

245

'I believe we have one somewhere,' she said, before proceeding to find it for me. 'A fascinating little volume,' she remarked brightly as she marked it down on the file.

I could hear her laughter as I went down the passage.

# 15

'I Know Now Who Did It . . .
But I Haven't a Vestige of Proof'

I had something to eat at The Three
Crows, and afterwards retired to my room
to study. I settled myself on the bed with
the diary, Pitman's book on shorthand,
and the letters Christie had so reluctantly
handed over to me.

I examined the letters first. A slender
bundle, fastened with an elastic band. I
slipped it off. The letters were addressed
to Christie, Poste Restante . . . So she had
been too cautious to send them to the
hospital.

The first one was dated vaguely:
*Tuesday, July*. It read:

*Darling — This is going to be a horrid
letter, What happened today must not
happen again ever, ever. I ought never
to have let you, but I couldn't help*

myself. I suppose it was a moment of weakness; but, darling, it must not happen again. You will have to be strong for me — and goodness knows you are strong enough. Darling, forgive me, and help me to be terribly brave and forget all about it. (Please burn this.) — Yours, NANCY.

The next was merely headed Thursday:

Never, never write to me here again, John — I thought you knew that. Suppose he had opened it? You must think of my point of view. I am sorry you feel the way you say you do about it, but I don't really see why you should blame me. It is just one of those things. I hope you will soon find yourself able to forget all about me — as I am sure you will if only you set your mind to it. — Yours sincerely, NANCY.

The next had been written on a Monday — presumably also in July. All the postmarks on the envelope were smudged and indecipherable.

248

*My own darling — How glad I am that our stupid quarrel is over! It was all my fault, whatever you may say. Let's not bother about it anymore. All I want to think about is this afternoon, and how sweet you were. Oh, sweetheart, I am just longing for tomorrow — but we must be careful. You will be sure to burn my letters, won't you, darling? I shall be thinking of you tonight. All my love and a hundred thousand kisses comes with this. And I shall make some excuse this evening to walk up to the village and see if you have written to me.*

*Don't forget Moppet and Poppet — Love, N.*

There were several more similar letters. It is not necessary to repeat them. The next one of interest was dated the twenty-somethingth of August, according to the postmark. She had again been content to write the day only.

*Oh, darling, are you absolutely sure nothing has gone wrong? I am so* dreadfully worried. I can't understand it. I thought we had been so careful, but whatever shall I do if I am right? I don't think I can be. I think it must just be the weather or something — and your silly old moppytop is making a fuss about nothing. Anyway, I'll let you know as soon as it's O.K., if I don't see you before. Thumbs up for me, sweetie. Moppet and Poppet send their love. And all mine, of course, from your silly old darling, N.

Dearest, I am sure something is wrong. I tried that stuff, you know, but nothing has happened; and, oh, I am so worried, darling. Do try and think of something quickly — if not, I don't know what I shall do. You know what a beast he is. If he found out, I don't know what he would do; but he would never forgive me, and never let me forget it, always probing away and trying to guess what you're thinking about and why . . . all that hateful stuff Darling, I don't mean to be wicked, but I think I'd rather die than he should find out. Why should I be the one to suffer? It's always the woman, isn't it? Darling, I don't mean to be horrid — I do love you — but it is your responsibility, too — isn't it? As much as mine. Do think of something to help your Anxious N, who loves you.

Sunday night.
Sweetheart — I'm sorry I've been such a beast to you all this time, but it's because I'm so wretched. But that's no reason to take it out on you, I know, because you have been sweetness itself, darling. Dr. Fortescue rang me up just now: she has come back from her holiday. I said I wanted to see her importantly, and so I do, darling. I have decided to ask her to help me. She is very fond of me, and I am sure she will. Of course, I do not mean to tell her anything about us, but shall say it is Maurice, naturally. I know it is dangerous, because she may say something to him or somebody else without meaning to. But, really, it seems like the only chance now short of actually

*murdering the beast. I am sure he is suspicious, darling: he has been looking at me so strangely these last few days, I shouldn't have been a bit surprised if he had said something. But, of course, he didn't. That's not his way. He just watches, and smiles his hateful smile to himself. I'm sitting opposite him now writing this. He ought to know, eh? Oh, how I wish you were here with me now to comfort me. Well, darling, think of me tomorrow going over the top; and, whatever happens, I am always your own darling,*

*N., who loves you.*

That was the last. If she had written again, he had either destroyed it or subtracted it from the packet before giving it to me. I sighed, and mixed myself a drink. There was a knock on the door. I called, 'Come.' And Trevor's cheerful countenance appeared.

'What have you got?' he said.

'Plenty,' I told him. I sat him in the armchair, and got him a drink. 'Enough for ten murders. What am I going to do with it all? There's too much instead of too little. But here's something for you: Nancy Royd was murdered!'

He let out a whistle of incredulity.

I told him as much as I knew myself. He sat spellbound.

'And now, just run your eyes over this little lot,' I said, passing him the letters. 'To use your favourite expression, it smells. I suppose you realise that the whole thing really hinges on whether Christie got that letter first thing Monday morning or not. We can wash him out as First Murderer if he did get the letter, because obviously he would wait to hear the result of her interview with Fortescue before bumping off the old man. But if he didn't get the letter — and I don't really see how he can have done in the time — then he is, to say the least of it, a consideration in this affair. She had been working herself and him into a fine state; that much is clear. Lord knows what she said to him when she was actually with him, but I don't suppose she was shy of piling it on. She seems to have been an adept at spinning a pretty tale. Well, what do you make of it?'

'Your guess is as good as mine.'

'Oh, it's not so bad. It's beginning to shape itself. If only I could get rid of some of these accursed suspects. But they lie so, both patients and staff. Which reminds me, can you do shorthand?'

'Yes. Not much speed now, but I could fudge up something. I worked my way up, you know, I'm not one of the young gentlemen from Hendon.'

'I meant, can you read it? I've found Mrs. Royd's diary, but she wrote it in shorthand, and it would take me years to unscramble — I've forgotten all mine. It will be a godsend if you can read it for me.' I handed it over to him.

'I may not be much good at puzzling out somebody else's outlines,' he said dubiously, 'but here goes.'

While he struggled with it, I prowled about the room restlessly.

At last he called over to me. 'Well,' he said, 'I may not have every word right, but it's near enough. I've left out all the gardening stuff.'

I sat down on the bed with his

transcription. He had started it at the first reference to Christie. It ran:

*A perfectly gorgeous young man begged me to play a game of tennis with him when I went up to the hospital this afternoon. I'd noticed him eyeing me before, and I rather wondered when he'd rise to it. He plays a fine game. Much too good for me. Of course, he asked me to play again, but I refused to be definite. I wonder what's wrong with him — he looks all right.*

Then, a few days later:

*Walking over to Nightingale Copse, who should I meet but my new flame. His name is John Christie. He really is rather a lamb. Absolutely dotty about me, bless him. A fast worker, too. Halfway through the copse he grabbed hold of me and kissed me — and how. Of course, I slapped him down good and hard. He grovelled beautifully, so I forgave him before we parted — when he promised he'd never do it again.*

*Met John by accident on purpose at Nightingale Copse. He's more in love with me than I thought, I'm afraid. He suddenly said he was absolutely mad about me, and if I wouldn't be his mistress he'd die, and all that sort of rot. Of course, I tried to tease him out of it. But he just went this ghastly colour and looked frightfully unhappy. And then he muttered goodbye and went away without looking at me again. I felt so dreadfully sony for him. Men get so awfully worked up about that sort of thing, and really it's so unimportant. It seemed too sad that he should be so unhappy when by doing a little act of kindness that meant absolutely nothing to me I could make him as happy as any man on earth. So I ran after him and fetched him back. The funny thing is that it wasn't till long after I'd left him that I remembered Maurice, and I realised that I'd been unfaithful to him. I suppose if he knew I'd never hear the end of it, and I'd have to listen to his 'interpretations' of that on top of all the rest. Why do* men make such a fuss about it? Well, I suppose now that I have remembered my duty at last, I shall have to write to John and call it all off. Damn!

Letter from John which made me furious, going off the deep end and so on. And the fool sent it here. Wrote back pretty stiffly. Maurice has been an absolute beast these last few days.

Went up to the hospital today and in the grounds ran into John. He was looking frightfully miserable, the poor lamb, and so handsome. The long and short of it was, of course, that we made it up. He really is a pet. Can't pretend that I feel very remorseful re Maurice. In the first place, this physical business doesn't mean much to me. Secondly, if it really is going to help this poor distressed sweet to get well again, I think it rates as a good action. Thirdly, I am quite well aware that Maurice is unfaithful to me, so what loyalty do I owe him in that direction? To be quite honest with myself, half the pleasure in *this is knowing that I'm getting a little of my own back. I must be careful, though; if he ever found out, it would lose its point, I'm afraid, and then some.*

*We really should find somewhere else to meet. Nightingale Copse is a darling spot, but in this hawk-eyed hamlet someone is sure to notice how often I go there, and then there'll be ructions. Might try Garrangarth. But getting there and back is a bore.*

*This is all very well, but I wonder where the dickens it is going to end. John, bless his heart, seems to be more and more dependent on me. He is adorable and awfully good fun, but I have no intention of running away with him, or getting Maurice to divorce me (which, of course, he would never dream of doing), as John keeps imploring me to do. For one thing, John has neither money nor job — nor any prospects either. A nice look-out that would be, I don't think! I imagine he will be well enough to leave in a month or two, and what is going to happen then? Supposing he won't go away, but tries to hang about me here? What a damnable mess! Oh, well, it's no use running to meet trouble, as Dad used to say. It'll probably have worn itself out by then.*

*I've got the wind up a bit. I hope it's only a false alarm. I'm late. We've always been careful, but, if the worst comes to the worst, I shall write to Joan Braithwaite for the address of that doctor who makes up that marvellous stuff that did the trick for her when Rupert ran out on her.*

*It looks as if I'm caught this time. Joan gave me the address all right, and I got the medicine; but I must be a lot tougher than Joan or something; anyway, it didn't do the trick for me. I feel as if I shall go crazy. And I'm a swine to John. Poor dear, he doesn't know whether he's on his head or his heels; can't make out what it's about at all. But it's all very well for him; I'm the one that has to pay the piper. Not so funny for me. Why do men get off scot-free? I wish to God now that I'd never seen John. And all this because I had a generous impulse!*

*I've made up my mind to tackle Mary as soon as she returns from her holidays. I'll get round her somehow. She's fond of me, and she can't stick Maurice. I wish she'd hurry back, though; the suspense is awful, and I'm afraid it will soon be too late. I have the most horrible idea that Maurice suspects something, too. He walked into the bathroom yesterday and absolutely stared at me as if he'd never seen me before. And he has really been most odd since then. Oh, if only this was all over!*

*Maurice is dead. I don't know how to write it. He has been murdered. He was hit with that heavy poker on the head. I feel . . . I don't know what I feel. I never meant that to happen. He* must have misunderstood me. How could he have thought I meant that? My brain feels absolutely numb; I can't think at all anymore. I suppose it's the shock. And yet I can't really pretend that I'm upset about Maurice. It's a ghastly way for it to have happened. But I never really cared for him, except that sort of glamour infatuation when I first met him. I think in some ways I hated him; he was so — unnatural. And I was frightened of him.

It's the other one now who's going to be an anxiety to me. Of course, it is absolutely essential that we hold no more communication until this has blown over. He must be sensible about this. He must realise that it is of the utmost importance.

Funny! I went up to see Mary this morning, and just when poor Maurice was — being killed — I must have been telling the most fearful lies about him. What an awful thought! Anyway, it availed me naught. To my surprise, she wouldn't budge an inch. But it doesn't matter now, thank God! The relief on that point is terrific. I feel a different person now that awful strain is ended. I feel ever so much happier about things generally now. I'm sure it will all come right in the end.

Of course, John had to behave like a perfect half-wit. Said he was worried about me and felt he had to ring me up just to enquire. He said it was perfectly safe, because he had went to Garrangarth to phone. I called him every name under the sun, and asked him if he did not realise that he was probably being followed, and that it would be the easiest thing in the world for them to check up on this phone call. He said he didn't realise anything of the sort. Why should anyone follow him? I said, 'I don't wish to discuss it. I'm going to ring off. Goodbye.' He threatened to ring me back, and to keep on ringing until I gave in and acted sensibly. Did I think he had done in the poor blighter, or what? he demanded. I thought I'd pass out then, but I managed to produce some faint reply.

Anyway, it appeared that it really was

not him. He swore it so indignantly that I believed him. And he was livid with me that I should have thought for an instant that he had. Aren't men funny? However, it's a great weight off my mind. All the same, I told him we must be very careful. Mustn't meet till this has blown over, and so on. To be suspected would not be at all funny, even if one knew one were innocent. I wonder, by the way, who did do it?

This morning a detective came to see me — not the funny little Inspector person that I saw before, but a private one working for Scotland Yard. I told him as much as I thought it safe for him to know, but he didn't look entirely satisfied. Why can't they leave it alone? It's done now.

I know now who did it. I suddenly absolutely knew it. But now comes the problem: what the devil am I supposed to do about it? I suppose legally I ought to inform the police, but I haven't a vestige of proof ... not a vestige of proof ...

That was the last entry.

'She knew who did it,' I said to Trevor. 'But she couldn't make up her mind whether to tell the police or not, damn it.'

'She might have saved her own life if she had told someone. Ironic, eh?' I remarked, bitterly. 'Cold-blooded little piece, wasn't she? There she was, seemingly a thoroughly nice, wholesome young girl, pretty as a flower. And then compare that picture of her with the letters to Christie, and compare the letters with the diary. Three different people. Just to think about it is enough to put you off women for life.'

'I'm a married man meself,' said Trevor, glumly.

'There you are! Look at you!'

'No need to insult me — ' He paused expressively. 'Of course, it's pique that she didn't have the forethought to mention who she believed to be the criminal and why.'

'I know who it is,' I said smugly.

'Then why the hell don't we arrest him?'

'Because I haven't a vestige of proof . . .'

# 16

## 'She Was Killed Because
## She Knew Too Much'

The inquest was held in the schoolroom of the village school. The coroner, fortunately, was a solicitor and knew his job. The public were not admitted; only the witnesses, the jurymen, the police and myself.

While the jurymen were being sworn in, I stared round the drowsy court with its drab walls, ornamented by a couple of out-of-date maps. A red-faced young policeman stood in the doorway, his hands behind his back, solemn with importance. I watched the motes dancing in the sunbeams from the window to the coroner's table. He moved a bundle of papers and opened the proceedings.

First in the agenda came Dr. Royd, of course. Written testimony from Mr. Martin, brief and to the point. Then

Sister Hythe deposed on finding the deceased. She stood there in a neat navy costume in a style of six years ago.

The foreman of the jury rose to his feet, and asked: 'Did you make sure that life was extinct?'

Sister Hythe gave a tight smile. 'There was no doubt of that.'

The coroner quickly moved on. Then followed in quick succession Dr. McIvor and the police. No loophole was given for questioning. The coroner's attitude brooked no larking about. He seemed to exude: 'It's an open and shut case.'

The witnesses examined, he summed up neatly and directed the jury to find their verdict.

The foreman stood up with an expression of luscious pomposity. 'We 'ave unanimously agreed to a verdict of wilful murder by a person or persons unknown.' He almost smacked his lips.

The coroner ordered an adjournment for luncheon.

The room was stuffy after lunch, and I looked longingly out of the window at the gold and blue day . . . I hoped we wouldn't take long with Mrs. Royd.

We opened with the maid's testimony. And then Dr. Fortescue was called. She looked pale but composed. I hoped to goodness we weren't going to drop any tiresome bricks about the night-call on the telephone.

Dr. Fortescue unemotionally described finding the body of her little friend.

'I understand,' said the coroner, 'that you are the doctor who performed the autopsy.'

Dr. Fortescue bowed her head. 'With the help of Dr. Blake. He did the analysis. I had nothing to do with that part.'

Dr. Blake was called and sworn. He was a dry and rather mannered little man. He was asked his findings as the result of the analysis. In a rapid, precise voice, he narrated a long and technically obscure rigmarole. The jury showed signs of strain. The coroner begged that it might be couched in simpler language.

'In effect,' admitted Dr. Blake, 'I found in the deceased's intestine and stomach nearly six grains of morphia.'

'Is that a lethal dose?' asked the

coroner, who knew the answer perfectly well.

Dr. Blake here attempted a long argument with himself to explain the action of morphia depending on the state of health and age of the person.

The coroner sighed. 'Have you any reason to believe that death was due to some other cause?'

'Oh, no.' Dr. Blake was emphatic. 'Death was certainly caused by morphine poisoning, taken orally. I only wanted to explain — '

'Quite, quite.'

So it went on . . . Witness after witness was called, dealt with, and despatched. But no word to show from where the poison was procured or how administered. Eventually the coroner summed up and the jury retired.

At length the foreman rose to his feet. The Coroner asked for the verdict.

'We would like to say that the deceased met her death by morphine poisoning, but that there is no proof as to 'ow it was administered. What we want is an open verdict, sir.'

I cursed softly. I supposed I could thank my stars that no more than that had come to light. And so could the hospital, the staff and the Committee.

Dr. Crawford stood in front of me. 'It's a farce,' she exclaimed indignantly.

'Oh, no! Very reasonable, really. We don't want everyone to know our business, do we? The good name of the hospital and so on. One murder is shockingly bad luck, two might seem like carelessness. And, people will think: if there are two, there are bound to be three . . . Three murders would be extravagant, don't you think?' I prattled.

She looked at me anxiously. 'When you go on like that, I don't know what to make of you.'

'Put your trust in God and keep your powder dry,' I advised. 'How about some tea?'

'You seem to do nothing but eat and drink,' she complained.

'Why this carping mood today? Surely you don't expect me to go tearing round the place grovelling on my stomach for invisible clues? Nowadays we use the little grey cells; we just lie back and think.'

'And then what happens?'

'Why, the psychological effect of that on the criminal is terrific. He daren't guess at how much the detective suspects and how much he knows. The suspense at length becomes intolerable. Maddened by the strain, the unhappy criminal flings himself on his knees and confesses all.'

'I wish you'd be serious,' Helen said. 'I want to talk to you. What have you found out? I know I ought not to ask, but since you told me it was murder, I've felt completely paralysed.'

'I've been able to check Christie's story, for one thing. It was as he said, more or less.' I gave her a brief résumé. 'The only point that baffles me is why she didn't pretend to her husband that the child was his; it seems such an obvious thing.'

'I suppose she lost her head. I can't feel so frightfully sympathetic about her now I know she was two-timing.'

'According to her, he was no lily either. Is that true?'

'You wouldn't expect me to know

about that, would you? It's hardly in my line,' she said with a wry smile. I begged her pardon.

'Which reminds me. Have you ever seen this before?' I passed the little red diary across to her. 'Does it mean anything to you?'

She thumbed the leaves curiously. 'I've never seen it before; but I believe I can tell you something about some of the entries. Here, for instance: 'Saw C 25, Saw C 100', etcetera . . . I happen to know that Chumly had been giving money to Royd for him to speculate with on his behalf. Royd was unlucky — at first, anyway — and I know Chumly was very worried and angry about it.'

I thanked her, and resolved to look into Royd's speculations.

And then, 'Excuse me a moment, please. I'll be back directly. I must see that man.' I hurried after Dr. Blake and caught him just as he stepped into his car.

'Just a minute, please,' I begged. I explained that I was working on behalf of Scotland Yard, and that I would be much obliged if he could help me on a few points.

'Be brief, please,' he said, brusquely. 'I have an appointment in Garrangarth in half an hour.'

'Did you find anything else in the stomach?'

He frowned. 'What were you thinking of particularly?'

I said, truthfully, 'I have no idea. I just thought there should have been something else, that's all. A hunch, shall we say?'

He threw me a peculiar glance. 'You are quite correct in assuming that there *should* have been something else in the stomach, but there wasn't. The stomach had been recently emptied. There were traces of mercury, though.' He looked at me slyly. 'Is that all?' He slipped the clutch.

'That's all, thank you, Doctor. That was just what I wanted to know.'

I could feel myself grinning as I went back to Helen.

'What is it?' she asked, curiously.

'I just asked him if he had found

anything else in the stomach,' I said. 'He hadn't.'

'Why is that good?' She frowned.

'Do you remember the incident of the dog in the night-time, my dear Watson?'

'Yes. But — '

'Apply it, my dear Watson. It is quite elementary, I assure you,' I chuckled.

'Oh, you are too tiresome for words today!'

'If you haven't guessed, I'll tell you as soon I've verified it myself,' I consoled her.

I went in search of Trevor, found him, and detached him deftly from a group of officials. All supplies of morphia at the hospital tallied all right, he told me, and none of the local chemists within a radius of ten miles had yielded so much as an unaccounted-for grain of the stuff. He looked depressed. 'Gawd knows where it came from,' he said.

'I have a pretty fair idea myself,' I said, modestly.

'Have you?' he said eagerly. 'Where?'

I repeated my conversation with Dr. Blake.

'I don't see the point. Anything to do with the mercury?' he said, vaguely.

'I don't know what the mercury means,' I confessed; 'chemistry is not my line. But surely, man, the significance of the rest strikes you? Look, we can safely assume that she took the capsules, since we have not found them anywhere. But no other drug — except for that trace of mercury — was in the body, beyond the morphia. We know from Chumly's evidence that she didn't take them while he was there. And I know, because I saw it myself, that Chumly's car was still there at eleven-thirty. Therefore, the capsules were taken after that. She then waited for them to pass into the stomach, and from thence they were evacuated. And at some time subsequent to all this she, knowingly or unknowingly, accepted about six grains of morphia, which had proved fatal by approximately eight o'clock in the morning.' I paused. 'Do you think that's a likely story? Because I think it's absolute balderdash.'

Trevor nodded. 'So the morphia was in the capsules, is that it?'

'So far as we know, only two people handled those capsules before Mrs. Royd — Dr. Chumly and Dr. Fortescue.'

'Good heavens!' said Trevor. 'Had either of them any motive?'

'You know as well as I do. There's not much doubt about it since we've read her diary. She was killed because she knew too much. So what we need to find is whether either of them had a motive for murdering Royd. Dr. Fortescue very much disapproved of him, that I do know. Chumly professes to have admired him. You pays yer money and yer takes yer choice.'

'There is still the little problem of the morphia. Where did they get it? It was not obtained locally.'

I slapped my thigh. 'Of course it wasn't,' I said. 'What a dumb cluck I've been! They have both been up to town recently. He to a medical conference, and she to a specialist with X-rays and all the trimmings. What more could you want?'

'I suppose you're telling me all this for some reason. You want me to handle it for you?'

'Please. We haven't got much to go on. They're not likely to have left any stray grains of morphia floating around for you to pick up with a search warrant. I think the thing to do here is to scare them into admitting something. It's no good my being gentle and polite and laying dainty traps for them. You need a large and very official-looking policeman for this part of the game.'

'I know. And he attacks them by telling them that he knows the truth already, that we've found the place they got the morphia from. Something like that, eh?'

I nodded enthusiastically. 'Go to it!'

# 17

## 'I Was Being Strangled'

*'Life is like a Mardi Gras. Funiculi, funicula-a-a!'* bellowed the gramophone. And a dozen couples trotted round the room. Just as if life really was like a Mardi Gras, I thought.

It was the night of the weekly dance at the hospital. It was a largish ballroom, with a fireplace at each end. The outer wall was a long glass window, the opposite a series of mirrors. The remaining wall-space was covered with cream paint. A grand piano stood in one corner, and on the other side of it was a radiogram with a cabinet of records. Little hard-backed chairs were ranged in groups at the edge of the floor, and an occasional alcove was filled by a stiffly formal sofa. The light fell from three ugly chandeliers.

The 'Ferry Boat Serenade' grated to

silence, and a vacuous-faced youth turned over the disc. The couples danced on without changing partners. '*Now's the time to roll the barrel* . . . ' sang some female in a polka-dotted voice.

'Yes, the gang's all here, all right,' said Barbara Harrison in my ear. 'How do you like 'em *en masse?*' she enquired.

I surveyed them. Many I knew by sight now, and with several I was on speaking terms: Miss Gellibrand, for instance, clasped in the arms of a small, perspiring man with a dramatic walrus moustache. Green stared over the head of his partner and hopped by.

'Why,' I asked Barbara, 'is he wearing white flannel trousers with a dinner jacket?'

She laughed. 'Association of ideas, perhaps . . . Empire building . . . playing the game . . . not cricket . . . You get the idea?'

Gresly and a very young girl swooped up and down the room with extravagantly gliding steps. Outside the windows I could see Croft pacing up and down, arm in arm with a young woman.

Someone put a waltz on the gramophone.

I turned to Barbara. 'Will you?' She slid into my arms, light as a feather.

As we whirled past an alcove, I saw that it was inhabited by Sister Hythe, wearing a long-sleeved lace frock of a virulent shade of arsenic-green. She sat primly on the edge of the yellow sofa, with a hideously set smile on her face that accentuated the watchful boredom of her eyes. Miss Gellibrand wandered across the room and sat down beside her, and at once engaged her in conversation. She gesticulated enthusiastically. I could see Sister Hythe was saying, 'Yiss, yiss,' and smiling, while her ferret eyes never ceased to rove round the room, watching . . .

Barbara said suddenly, 'Have you lost your heart to the Glamorous Hythe? You haven't taken your eyes off her for the last ten minutes.'

'Passing over that slight exaggeration, I do find her fascinating. I think it's the combination of arsenic-green on canary-yellow. I have never seen anything like it on land or sea.'

'Expressive of her nature, you know.

With the character of a leopard — always on the pounce.'

Martin danced by us just then, his partner's face hidden from me. Then he turned the corner, and I saw that the girl was Miss Wylie.

'What do you think of her?' I whispered to Barbara. 'I heard my glamorous Hythe going at her hammer and tongs the other day. Is that usual?'

Her black eyes sparkled. 'Tell me more. I dearly love a bit of gossip.'

'No, no. I'm asking for information, not giving it,' I said firmly.

At this point the record ended. We leant against the wall and watched them take partners for 'The Chestnut Tree'.

Arm in arm, they skipped down the room . . . Miss Gellibrand, oozing 'go' and self-conscious jollity from every pore, capered along with the empty-faced boy who had been attending to the gramophone . . .

' . . . *and the blacksmith shouted,* '*CHESTNUTS!*' . . . ' they carolled.

There was something horribly gruesome about it. The imbecile words, the gaily absurd gestures executed with such precision, accorded ill with the sombre and vacant expressions of the majority of the dancers. Like funeral mutes, their countenances suitably drawn for a pavane, they skipped around light-heartedly, picking their way faultlessly through all the movements.

'It's horrid, isn't it?' said Barbara sympathetically.

Once more the jigging rhythm of the 'Ferry Boat Serenade' vibrated in my ears. I saw Martin sidle towards us. He turned to me and said in a low voice that he would like very much to speak to me. I indicated the wide open spaces outside. I opened the French windows and trickled through after him. I was aware of Sister Hythe's watchful eyes picking curiously at my back.

Martin said, 'I suddenly remembered something, and I thought it might be important, so I came to tell you just as soon as I found you.'

'Very sensible of you,' I told him. 'Talk away.'

'You know I told you that I didn't know

what I was doing during those minutes I was alone? Well, I was standing by Dr. Royd's desk — staring down at him sprawled across it, you see — and under one of his hands was a pad of paper, that he had been writing on just before it happened. I must have been staring at that in the meaningless, unseeing way one does . . . And now, after all this time I can suddenly see those written characters before me . . . so clearly that I can read what they say. It's quite a common trick of the subconscious to register things automatically so that they can be reproduced consciously later . . . '

'And you can reproduce this for me now?' I asked eagerly.

He nodded. 'I'll write it down for you.' He led me to the writing room. He took a slip of paper and a pencil. Thoughtfully, he wrote:

> *Pankhurst,*
> *great reluctance I feel compel*
> *you of certain facts that I*
> *concerning Dr. McIvor. It has*
> *that a patient of his, by name*

*att, an inmate of this hospital*
*to the dispensary and obtained*
*unobserved. The dispenser on*
*severely reprimanded and much to*
*though Miss Pratt unfortunately*
*Dr. McIvor himself signed the*
*cate, and replaced the miss*
*stock. These are the facts of*
*to make the decision . . .*

'That was all I could see,' said Martin as he handed me the paper. 'His hand covered one part and his body the other. I can't make head or tail of it, but it may be useful to you . . .'

'I'm very grateful,' I said. 'This *will* be very useful to me. You haven't mentioned this to anybody else, have you? No? Well, don't, as much for your own health as anything else. Try and forget the whole thing now . . . Coming back to the ballroom?' I remembered that Lord Pankhurst was a member of the Committee.

The Palais Glide was in progress. In rows of ten or twelve they swung round the room.

I checked my watch. Ten o'clock. I might as well go back to the local. In any case, they would be ending soon now.

The sweet-faced Miss Wylie let out a sudden howl and started clawing her arms wildly. Sister Hythe went over to her, and said something softly. Whereupon Miss Wylie dissolved into a cascade of hysterical tears and suffered herself to be led from the room, supported by Hythe, who was half her size.

With aristocratic indifference they danced on . . .

'Too much excitement,' explained the omnipresent Mrs. Harrison. 'It's so easy for them to get overstimulated, and then something 'goes', of course.'

'And nobody gives a damn.'

'Oh, yes, they do,' she contradicted me, 'but it just isn't the thing to pay any attention publicly to other people's misfortunes. Besides, it happens so much that one really does become inured to it . . . It's an embittering experience, you know,' she admitted sadly.

I felt a profound urge to help her. 'You'll come through all right,' I said vehemently. 'Just you hang on, and mark my words . . . I'm going now. Goodnight.'

I hummed to myself as I strolled down the hillside towards The Three Crows. A patter of running footsteps echoed in the quiet night. I stopped and strained my eyes in the darkness, for the moon had not yet risen. The running footsteps came on. Dimly, I could discern a heavier opaqueness that stumbled with sobbing breath towards me. I caught it in my arms. It let out a stifled shriek and then gasped out, 'Oh, Jacob, is it you?'

I was startled. 'Helen, for God's sake, what are you doing here? Are you all right?'

She leant against me. 'I am now, I think. But don't leave me just yet, please.' She was gasping for breath.

'Do you feel able to walk with me as far as The Three Crows? You could sit there and have a drink and get your breath,' I suggested.

'I can't go there,' she said, 'I'm all — well, I must be dishevelled, anyway. It would be a fearful scandal if I went in there all topsy-turvy . . . '

'Hang on a minute,' I said suspiciously. 'I'm going to have a look at you.' I found my torch and played the thin beam on her face.

What I saw made me exclaim wordlessly. Her hair, in a wild tangle, stood out in a fierce halo round her face. Two long scratches ran down her left cheek, and blood dripped down her chin from a cut lower lip.

'My dear,' I said foolishly, 'have you had an accident?'

'No, it was on purpose,' she said grimly. 'Jacob, I'm feeling rotten. Take me home, will you, please? I'll tell you all about it there. I simply dare not go through the grounds alone again . . . I'm awfully sorry to be a nuisance.'

'Don't be silly,' I scolded her. 'Take my arm. And don't talk: you'll need all your breath.'

I got her back to the cottage, sat her down in an armchair, and fixed her a stiff drink. 'Get that down yourself,' I said firmly, 'and then you can tell me your story — when you can.'

I was shocked at her appearance. Her

suit was crumpled and muddied, with bits of fern and twig adhering to it. Her legs were covered with abrasions, and all that was left of her fine silk stockings were a few web-like threads that bound the gaping holes together. A tousled yellow silk scarf trailed across her shoulder. She leant her head back wearily against the cushions, and I saw that her neck was reddened and bruised in long streaks . . .

Colour was slowly flooding back into her cheeks.

'Hadn't you better clean your wounds, Helen, before you settle down to tell me about it? I'll help — '

'I can do it,' she said, and left the room. She came back bearing a small bowl full of colourless fluid and carrying a roll of cotton wool. She set them on a small table beside her, tore off a lump of wool, dipped it in the fluid and took up a small hand-mirror.

'My God, what a ghastly sight!' She dabbed energetically at the blood drying on her chin, and cleaned up her cut lip. She worked in silence as I waited patiently.

Eventually, she said: 'Someone attacked me. You realise that, don't you? They — '

'Wait,' I interrupted. 'Please start at the beginning.'

She smiled for the first time. 'Omitting no detail, however trifling it may seem. All right, Holmes . . . I thought I'd go to bed early for once, and so round about ten o'clock I went upstairs to my room . . . I never put my bedroom shutters up until I go to bed. So tonight, I walked into my dark room, and went over to the window to put up the shutters before turning on the light. It seemed a lovely night, and idly I stuck my head out of the window. I was just sniffing the air, and wondering whether it was going to rain tomorrow, when I saw a flicker of light come from the direction of the little wood. I paid no attention — anyone might have been strolling round there, maybe lighting a cigarette. Next time I looked in that direction, the light flickered — on and off; on and off — twice, whilst I watched.' She was washing some of the mud off her hands and sucking her breath in sharply when the antiseptic stung the raw places.

'That seemed a little odd to me,' she continued. 'I suppose one hears so much about spies nowadays, and Fifth Columnists . . .

'I watched it for a while. Dark for a few minutes, and then the light would flash up and flicker on and off . . . I waited, half-expecting to see a fleet of planes come sweeping silently down in answer . . . It seemed to be signalling of some description, and the thought came to me that I ought, perhaps, to do something about it. The police? No, they were so far away; and it was probably nothing really, just one of the more thoughtless patients playing the fool. That decided me. I flung a scarf round my neck, and went off in the direction of the flickering, beckoning light.' She rolled the remnant of stocking down her leg, and proceeded to deal with her grazed knee.

'I had only gone a few yards from the house when the light went out for good. Did that mean the signaller's job was over, and that he or she had gone away? Or did it mean that he or she had heard me coming? I determined to see the thing through to the end. I walked on as quietly as I could, till I came to the edge of the little wood. Then I waited and listened; but not a sound except for the night birds and the rustle of leaves in the breeze.'

She sat back and stared at me tensely. 'I had no idea which way to take then, so I just walked straight ahead. And then, without warning . . . something dropped on me out of the sky . . . or out of nowhere . . . something tremendously heavy, it was. It caught me full in the back, and knocked me to my knees . . . I was absolutely stunned at first. I should think people must feel very like that when they're shot. And then I couldn't breathe properly . . . I felt an agonising pain round my neck . . . I wanted to put my hand up to my throat, but it seemed too difficult . . . and then I became conscious that whatever it was that had struck me was still weighing on my back; that, in fact, it was a person and not a thing. That galvanised me; my brain suddenly began to work once more . . . Of course, all this could really only have lasted about five seconds, though it takes longer to tell

. . . I became fully aware then that I was choking, that I was being strangled . . .

'I gathered all my strength together, and flung myself backwards and twisted as I landed . . . My assailant must have been taken by surprise, for the constriction about my throat gave way. And now I was in the advantageous position. But only for an instant, for with astonishing strength I was hurled to one side . . . a knee was thrust sharply into my stomach, and I felt the two ends of my scarf being drawn tighter and tighter . . . I remember a curious buzzing in my head, and the blood was drumming in my ears. I had some confused notion that it was the invasion bells, and that I'd been too late, after all, and was going to die for nothing . . . That made me wild again, and I had another spurt of energy . . .

'I don't remember what happened in sequence . . . I only remember fighting desperately with someone who seemed to possess the strength of a demon . . . Stumbling over roots . . . hurtling into trees . . . And then somehow I broke free from those awful clawing hands, and with every ounce of strength I had left, I started running . . .

'All I wanted to do was get away . . . And when I found myself somehow on the road to the village, I kept on running. I thought if only I could get to you, you would — you would know what ought to be done . . . ' Her voice trailed into silence.

I stood there, staring down at her and visualising the whole scene. I felt a cold, leaden knot at the base of my stomach when I thought of what might have happened. Helen unprepared, unarmed and alone, at the mercy of a cold-blooded ruthless murderer who had successfully struck twice . . .

I took her hand in mine. 'I want to apologise for falling down on the job like this,' I said, miserably. 'When I think of the danger you were in, I feel sick . . . '

'Don't be absurd!' she admonished me, pulling a comb jerkily through her matted curls. 'How could you have helped it?'

'I couldn't, as it happened, but I should have been able to . . . That's what I'm here for, you know. What kind of a detective am I, with people being murdered left and right under my very nose?'

'Now, dear, there's no need to exaggerate,' she said, blinking at me like a friendly owl as she polished her glasses with the edge of her crumpled scarf. 'Don't take it to heart so, Jacob. There's no harm done. And accidents will happen.'

'Accidents be damned! What would I be feeling like now if you were lying at my feet, a bleeding corpse? The least I could have done was to have warned you that something like that might happen, only it didn't occur to me. Quick-witted Chaos, that's me. Anyway, I expected you to have more sense than to go chasing about after hypothetical spies.'

'Ah now, don't start bullying me tonight, for God's sake, or I shall burst into tears,' she pleaded. 'Let's skip the rest, shall we? Obviously you never meant it to happen. It was, as you so rightly remarked, my own idiotic fault. No one except the murderer is going to know anything about it, and your reputation is unsmirched.'

'I wasn't thinking about my reputation — to hell with that — '

She looked at me slyly. 'Were you thinking of me, then? Was that what was worrying you?'

'You know it was,' I said uncomfortably.

'Well, don't look so sulky about it, my pet. I take it very civil of you to be so concerned. What is worrying you? Are you feeling — '

I put my hands on her shoulders. 'None of that,' I said sternly. 'Don't you play the psychiatrist with me, madam. I'll *show* you what I'm feeling.' And, so saying, I pressed my mouth on hers . . .

'I've been wanting to do that for a long time,' I said eventually.

'You might have considered my wounds,' she said composedly, dabbing at her mouth. And then she smiled and slipped her cool hand into mine. 'You're a comfortable sort of creature, Jacob.'

'Is that the best you can do as a profession of love?'

'N-no. But please — don't be difficult . . . I do feel rather off-balance and

— erratic, emotionally, tonight,' she stammered. 'Do try and understand me . . . I'm trying to hold on to myself.'

'You're a plucky woman,' I said admiringly. 'May I mix you another drink?' I mixed two and carried them back to her.

I sat myself on the floor by her chair. Helen gently tugged at a convenient lock of my hair. 'Go ahead. I'm at your disposal,'

'Thank you. Then let us go back to your playful pal of the wood. Of course, you couldn't see who it was, but I expect you can tell me something about him — or her. Which was it, by the way?'

She said slowly, 'I can't be sure. Of course, my brain was not working at its best exactly, and I think I just took it for granted that it was a man. Now it occurs to me that it might have been a woman.'

'You mean that you didn't actually feel a beard on this person; but, on the other hand, you didn't feel ringlets or a bun, shall we say?'

'Exactly. Mind you, I still think the probability is that it was a man. All I know is that it was a large, lumpy creature, very heavy and strong, wearing some thick rough tweed . . . and smelling faintly of iodoform, I think,' she said hesitantly. 'But the scent of the pine needles was so much stronger that I can't be absolutely certain about that either. Sorry. I'd be a rotten detective, wouldn't I?'

'Just remember to take your notebook with you next time . . . Well now, you say this person jumped on you from behind. I don't quite see . . . Look, do you feel strong enough to go in for a little reconstruction? I'll try not to be too violent.'

She nodded, and I pulled her to her feet and pushed the furniture back against the walls.

'O.K. Now you come along past me here . . . slowly, like you did at the time . . . '

I lunged at her as she passed, but misjudged my distance, and there was no force in it.

'Just where did the main weight fall? Do you think he grabbed you low, in a flying tackle?'

'Oh, no,' she said. 'I took all the weight on my shoulders.'

She walked by again, and I threw myself as high as I could. But Helen was only about four or five inches shorter than I; and, although she stumbled under the impact, she said it was not right. I frowned. Something was wrong. The man would have to be about eight feet high . . . Eight feet high!

I snapped my fingers. 'He didn't jump on you at all, Helen. He *dropped* on you. That was the expression you used yourself, remember? He dropped on you, out of a tree. Of course it knocked you to your knees; the wonder is that it didn't knock you out completely. And do you get the significance of it?' I went on excitedly. 'What was he doing up in a tree? He was sitting there waiting for you to pass underneath. So he knew you were coming. Doesn't that sound as if those signals were for you? Not for you to understand, but for you to investigate. A trap, in fact.'

'And I walked slap into it,' said Helen bitterly.

'Yes; but why *you*? Why are you a danger? What important fact have you got up your sleeve? It must be something vital to the solution of the mystery.'

'I haven't got anything up my sleeve,' she said indignantly.

'It might be something you've forgotten, or which the point of has not yet struck you. But whatever it is, Helen, I wish you'd hurry up and think of it. Not only for my benefit, but for your own. Once you've remembered and told it, you're safe from further attacks. So *think*, there's a good girl, *think* . . . Meanwhile, if it's all the same to you, we'll be getting on with the reconstruction to see what else we can discover about this chap. Do you mind getting down on the floor in the same position you were in after he first struck you . . . ?'

She twisted her scarf round her neck, put her glasses on the mantelpiece, and obediently knelt down in a crouching posture in the middle of the floor.

'I see. Yes, it would be like that, I imagine. And then I am sort of hanging round your neck like so. Is that right?

Good! Then what happened?'

'Then I lurched forward with all my weight, like this . . . '

'That didn't throw me off my balance. But that may have been because I was expecting it. Besides, I'm a pretty hefty chap. All right, we'll take that as done . . . I've fallen back like this, eh? I see, then you twist round . . . And I take the ends of your scarf . . . '

Helen's face was very close to mine. I could see minute feathery yellow stripes in the grey iris of her eyes, and my own intent reflection in her dilated black pupils . . . I moved my face so that her cheek rested on mine . . . The lovely weight of her body was on mine, and I could hear her heart beating with slow, heavy thuds . . .

She rubbed her cheek caressingly against mine, and leant away from me with a faint, sweet smile. I said: 'When I've cleared up this mess — '

'I don't believe the thing will ever come to an end, Jacob . . . And in some horrible way, I don't really want it to end . . . I'm afraid, dreadfully afraid, of what is going to happen . . . I feel something absolutely devastating is pending . . . God, Jacob, I wouldn't admit this to anyone but you, but I'm terrified. Who's going to be next? Supposing it's you . . . '

'Darling, you're just being silly. You're overwrought, and no wonder . . . '

'Don't say I'm hysterical,' she warned, her voice harsh with strain. 'I daresay I'm only speaking like this because I've had a beastly shock, but it has only released what was there all the time. Deep down inside, I'm shaking with fear when I think about it all . . . I wish to God you'd drop it, Jacob,' she cried passionately, and her eyes were wide with fear.

I lifted her to her feet and drew her to me. Holding her face between my hands, I said very solemnly, 'Darling, I swear to you by all that is most dear to me, that nothing would induce me to pass up on this until I have found the murderer and handed him over. I mean that, Helen. Even if they took me off it officially, I would still work at it privately. It's a dirty case, darling, and whoever did it is not going to get away with it while Jacob

Chaos walks the earth. You go and catch some decent sleep — it's after two — and you'll feel a different woman tomorrow.'

She stared at me for a while, and then said, 'Yes, I am very tired. Goodnight, Jacob.'

I bent over her. 'Goodnight, Helen darling. See you tomorrow. Sleep well.'

'Yes. Come and dine with me here,' she said, and turned away.

As I walked home, I tried to sort out my impressions, but I felt so sleepy that it was all a confused muddle . . .

Six grains of morphia . . . Dr. Fortescue's visit to London, and Dr. Chumly's ditto . . . Dr. Royd's letter to the Committee concerning Dr. McIvor . . . A faint trace of mercury . . . A flickering light . . . The mysterious assailant . . . Open verdict . . . Sister Hythe on the yellow plush sofa . . . Helen's yellow scarf.

Somewhere in all that lay a clue, some trifle that eluded my sleep-dulled senses . . . *Tomorrow I'll remember*, I promised myself . . . forgetting that it already *was* tomorrow.

With some difficulty, I roused the landlord of The Three Crows. And with stolid unamiability he pulled back the heavy bolts to let me in. He didn't say a word.

Upstairs in my room, I found a note on my bedside table. It was from Trevor, and ran:

*Thought you'd like to know that the Fortescue has a nice little quantity of dope in her bottom drawer. Says it was her own private store — I bet it was — and that she didn't have to tell me what it was for. When tackled with my well-known verve and aplomb, she went to pieces — more or less — and admitted that about six grains were missing. Yes, you were right, she did get them while she was in London.*

*I told you the case stank, didn't I? I shall be paying you a formal call tomorrow morning, maestro. Goodnight.*

One more river, one more river to cross . . . I looked at myself glumly in the glass.

I could hear Dr. Fortescue saying, 'Who could help believing in God on a day like this?' And again I saw the sun silvering her grey hair and showing up the lines of fatigue on her large, white face. I sighed and crawled into bed. *I won't think about it anymore tonight*, I told myself, *I'll think of Helen*. But instead I fell asleep . . .

# 18

## 'We Don't Want Any More *Accidents*, Do We?'

As promised, Trevor came up in the morning. We got down to things right away. I told him about Mr. Martin's usefully retentive subconscious.

'That rather gums up the works, don't it?' he remarked. 'Well, don't smile in that maddeningly superior fashion.'

'All right. This is how it is. The actual letter that Royd wrote has not been seen by anyone official. But McIvor admits having taken charge of it, together with the rest of Royd's papers. When I asked him for it, he fumbled about and pretended he'd mislaid it or some such nonsense. I suppose he has destroyed it. But why, if McIvor murdered Royd to prevent him sending that letter to the Committee, did he not remove it then and destroy it? Why leave it for Martin or

304

anyone else to read, and only remove it afterwards when he was called to the scene of the crime by Sister Hythe? S'logic, see?'

He nodded. 'Easy enough when you know. Anything more up your sleeve?'

'Something much jollier.' I grinned maliciously. And I recounted the story of the murderous attack on Dr. Crawford. When I had finished, we looked at each other in grim silence.

'So now we know,' I muttered ironically. 'Lord knows when this case is going to break open, and all I ask of you is to be ready when I need you. You can understand just how tough it may be. We don't want any more *accidents*, do we?'

'Trust Trevor,' he said solemnly. 'One thing is rather puzzling me, though. Why did Mrs. Royd want Dr. Fortescue to come down to her that night? She knew who the murderer was . . . or thought she did. She might have been wrong,' he mused, 'but in that case, why was she killed? Lord, what a mad muddle! Anyway, if she did know it was Dr. Fortescue, why did she want to see her so particularly that night? She must have realised the risk she was running. I can't understand why she didn't leave a note of some description. Or even a sign. Have you searched the house thoroughly?'

'Not a stick left unturned. It is a puzzle, I agree. I might have another look around, but I don't think it will be any use.'

We discussed further plans in greater detail, and finally parted with mutual expressions of civility and esteem.

Downstairs in the lounge I saw Barbara Harrison and Boney, knocking back brandies with a faintly guilty, conspiratorial air.

'Hullo, chaps,' I called.

'Come on over,' said Barbara, beckoning. 'We're playing hookey, you know, and have come down here to be frightfully mad and bad — and then later, I expect, we'll be sad . . . What'll you have?'

Boney went over to fetch the drinks.

Barbara turned to me. 'I'm not such a lunatic as I seem,' she assured me. 'It's Boney. He'd got one of his spells on him, and I didn't mean to let him run wild alone. I thought if I came with him I could keep an eye on him, and also try to keep down the consumption to some extent. You see, his doctor is on holiday just now, and he feels abandoned and at a loose end. Then, you know, one gets to feel thoroughly low and disconsolate, and so one slips back to one's old bad habits . . . '

'What's his trouble?'

'Chronic alcoholism,' she said with a grimace. 'Poor chap! But what the hell! If it's not one thing, it's another.'

Boney came back with the drinks. She splashed in the soda liberally, and took a long pull at hers.

I said, 'Tell me, I can't make out quite what is supposed to happen here. What is the treatment really? How does it work?'

'That depends a lot on the case. There is deep analysis, like I suffered from Royd. You say anything that comes into your head, and then he tells you some perfectly foul reason why you said it. Then you feel either crushed or indignant. If you feel crushed, you don't dare talk anymore, and just sit there in gloomy silence. Or, if you feel indignant, you have a gory row about it, which he wins. Either way, you feel like hell afterwards. My own idea about it is that they like to make life such a living hell here that the outside world will seem a bed of roses in comparison,' she added with a laugh.

'I must be honest, though, and admit that some people really enjoy it. Then there is the light therapy,' she continued, 'a lot of auto-suggestion and pep-talk . . . Then there's free-association, that's used a lot. And dream-analysis, of course, all the doctors simply dote on it. Oh, and I mustn't forget all the jolly little things like evipan and hypnosis . . . and scopolamine.' She shuddered. 'I think that's hitting below the belt, myself. They wanted me to have it when I first came, but not Pygmalion likely.'

'What is it?'

'Don't you ever read the papers? Haven't you heard of what they call the truth-drug in America? They use it on criminals to get at the truth. It gets rid of your thingumabob and all the scum rises to the top, see? It puts to sleep the conscious part of you that is always on guard, keeping down the dangerous thoughts and memories, in other words. And it doesn't put you right off to sleep, you can still talk and answer questions — but all your murky subconscious is released, and you can't defend yourself and lie or anything like that. It's like hypnosis.

'Of course, they don't use it much. Most of them prefer it all to come out naturally. But they have to use it sometimes with the bad ones — the ones who are very sick, the ones that *won't* talk, or the ones that are overexcitable and hysterical — to quiet them down and relieve them if they're overwrought, and so on . . . ' she explained, and drained the last of her drink.

Boney said, 'Have another drink, darling.'

'No, sweet. No more. We must get back and find some lunch. Otherwise they'll be sending the bloodhounds out for us.'

Illumination burst on me like a starry rocket. I stood up. 'I must go,' I said. Deep in their argument, they scarcely remarked on my departure.

I cut across the fields to the hospital.

I poked my head in the porter's cubby-hole. 'May I have a look at the appointment book?' I said.

He passed it over without a word — civil or otherwise.

I turned back the leaves of the heavy ledger . . . found the page I wanted . . . ran my finger down . . . *Ah!* There we were . . . Miss Wylie . . . Just as I thought.

I closed the book with a bang and handed it back. 'Where can I find Miss Wylie at this hour?'

He stared at me discourteously. 'Couldn't say, sir, I'm sure.'

'What number is her room?'

He allowed me that, and I went up. Fortunately, she was in. In two minutes, I had learnt what I wanted to know.

# 19

### 'The Murderer is a Doctor'

I was about to leave the hospital when I saw Dr. Ennis running toward me down the corridor, his chubby face pale and drawn. He gripped me by the arm.

'What is the matter with this place, Mr. Chaos . . . ? You'd better come along, too, I think . . . It's as if there were some frightful contagious disease spreading over the place . . . The hospital will be ruined . . . ruined . . . ' He dragged me along after him.

'What's happened?' I asked.

He pulled me over to a window and pointed. Far below in the courtyard I could see a group of people bending over a something — a something lying on the flagged paving. I could see McIvor and Chumly and two sisters. The porter and the nurse came round the edge of the building, carrying a stretcher.

I said: 'Who is it? I thought it was impossible to jump out of windows here with all these bars and things.'

'Theoretically, it is,' Ennis said wearily, moving away. 'I suppose he must somehow have got on the roof over by those farcical ramparts. It is quite possible to get through on that side, but you wouldn't expect a patient to know that.'

'Is he dead or only injured?'

'Oh, God, dead from that height. Good-looking kid, too. I thought he was going to be discharged in a week or so. A young man called Christie.'

Christie! I felt as though somebody had kicked me in the pit of the stomach. Just a few minutes on the wrong side of the ledger. Just a little speed-up somewhere, and the whole thing could have been prevented and a life saved. For surely I could have saved his life — given foresight and a tiny extra span of time. I cringed at my own incompetence.

They had brought him in and laid him on the couch in the dispensary. All the doctors were there. Helen — looking as sick as I felt — remarked: 'He was my patient.' Her whisper was an agony of self-reproach.

Chumly finished what he was doing by the body, straightened up, and caught my eye. 'I have to speak to you.'

We went over to the far end of the room by the window, and stood with our backs to the others. He spoke in a low voice, staring out through the pane.

'I have a confession to make,' he began. 'You remember the night of Mrs. Royd's death? I was the last person to see her alive, so far as we know. Anyway, I must have been the last person she expected to see that night, because just as I was leaving she came running after me and thrust a letter into my hand. Would I post it for her, please, it was very important. I told you before, she was rather excited. So as to be sure not to forget it, I stuck it in the pigeon-hole of my dashboard where I keep my driving gloves. I'm afraid I've a shocking memory. I *did* forget. But today I put my hand into the back for something, and — I found it . . . A letter addressed to Christie, Poste Restante . . . Then I remembered. I thought, you know, it would surely be too much of a coincidence for it to be anyone but the Christie at the hospital — I knew she knew him, for I had seen them talking together — so to make up for my carelessness, I brought it up here at once . . . '

'Where is it?' I asked quickly.

'I gave it to Christie,' he said miserably. 'I thought I had better tell you, in view of what has happened, because it would seem as though — as though it did have some bearing on the — the accident. I suppose I should really have given it to you in the first place. It's too late now to say *I didn't think*; and what is the use of saying *Sorry* . . . ?' His voice died away, and he licked his dry lips.

I had not time for him just then. I was out of the dispensary and upstairs in Christie's room in a few strides. Like the other rooms, it was bare, with ugly, meagre furniture. There were not many places to look. On the bedside table was a freshly-written letter.

*TO WHOM IT MAY CONCERN,*
*I am going to kill myself, now, as*

314

soon as I have written this, because I killed Dr. Royd, and I am responsible for Mrs. Royd's death. The detective will tell you why I killed him. It was quite easy. I missed part of Occupations that Monday morning because I had cut my hand tree-felling. It seemed to me a very good opportunity. There was a lot of blood from my wound, and I thought that would conveniently account for any accidental splashes. They told me in the dispensary to go and lie down. I said I would, but instead I went down the passage, through the communicating door, and killed him with the poker. At the time it seemed a wise move. I never meant Mrs. Royd to die too. I apologise for all the trouble I have caused; but I think this is the only way out for me.

JOHN CHRISTIE

I had no intention of having this broadcast in the dispensary in front of all the nurses, so I suggested to McIvor that he and his colleagues adjourn as soon as might be to some convenient room where we could talk undisturbed.

I waited while chairs were fetched, and they arranged themselves about McIvor's consulting room: Chumly, McIvor behind his own desk, Mary Fortescue, Ennis, Helen, and myself standing in the centre of the room. Then I handed McIvor the letter.

He read it through first, and then aloud to the others. I watched their faces.

'Well, that is the end, thank God.' McIvor's tone was heartfelt.

'Has anyone a specimen of his handwriting?' I asked. 'I must just check up on it to make sure it really is his.'

Dr. Crawford nodded and left the room, to return in a few minutes with a file which she handed to me. It contained the notes on his case, and in it were several handwritten descriptions of his dreams. The writing looked to be his, all right.

'There you are,' I said. 'Practically, that ends the case. There remains for you the problem of how you are going to hush up all this affair so that as little as possible leaks out to scandalise the general public.'

Dr. McIvor said, stolidly, 'I am sure we shall all be most interested to hear Mr. Chaos's report on the case. There are many points that are still quite obscure — to me, anyway.'

I looked down. 'I must admit . . . I feel I have failed lamentably — '

Helen jumped in: 'You're embarrassing us all most frightfully, Mr. Chaos. We know the difficulties under which you had to work. And I at least can vouch for your hard work on the case.'

This kindly speech was accompanied by an obbligato of shuffling and awkward murmurs.

'Thank you, Doctor. I would like to take this opportunity to thank you for the truly invaluable assistance you have given me.' I turned to the others. 'Without Dr. Crawford's help, I might never have solved the case. I use the word 'solve' advisedly, because, as I mean to show you, I did solve it — just a few minutes before I learnt of Christie's death and the confessional letter he left behind.'

I began to explain to them from the

beginning all the boring verification of statements, the testing of alibis, and so on. Gradually, the elimination of suspects narrowed down the list. We came to Mrs. Royd's death. I had had no doubt from the first that it was murder. Then the attack on Dr. Crawford. That narrowed the possibilities still further. I had the final but central clue only that morning, and I had hurried up at once — just too late to prevent the murderer striking for the third time.

'The third time!' exclaimed McIvor, his face grey. 'Christie committed suicide. What do you mean?'

Consternation reigned. Chumly buried his face in his hands. Ennis got up and walked to the window. The two women sat as rigid as iron — only Mary's hands clasped and trembled in her lap, and Helen's eyes were closed.

'We don't know that Christie committed suicide,' I reminded McIvor gently. 'We only know he left a note to say he *intended* to commit suicide, and that he was later found dead from injuries caused by falling from a considerable height.

That is not entirely satisfactory proof.'

Dr. Ennis looked at me thoughtfully. 'It would take a pretty strong man to chuck Christie out of a window against his will.'

'A good point,' I agreed. 'Still, when I tell you what Dr. Chumly told me a little while ago, I think you will admit that there is something to be said in favour of my assumption. You see, he had just received a letter from Mrs. Royd, a letter which I have good reason to believe contained the murderer's name. Mrs. Royd believed she knew who had killed her husband. Whether she was shielding them or whether she never had time to tell us who she suspected, I don't know. I presume she had guessed all or a dangerous part of the truth, since she was killed. And I believe that she sent at least part of this information in a letter to John Christie, which Dr. Chumly forgot to deliver until today.'

'I don't believe it,' said Chumly, passionately. 'I never mentioned a word about that letter to a single living soul except yourself. How *could* the murderer know anything about it, much less what was in it?'

'What *was* in it?'

'How the hell should I know?' he snarled.

'It does seem a trifle coincidental,' murmured Dr. Fortescue, 'that the murderer should turn up at the very convenient moment when Christie had a letter accusing him, and that he was able to get hold of this, persuade Christie to write a farewell letter, and then either push him or persuade him to jump off the roof, all without giving Christie a chance to scream for help or defend himself or anything.'

'It does give one food for thought,' I agreed, 'and leads one to some strange conclusions. But let us leave that for the time being. Let us examine the psychology of the protagonists.

'Firstly, one curious thing about the murders is that superficially they have nothing in common. The first murder was a most brutal crime, the sort of unpremeditated act one would *expect* to find occurring among a set of unbalanced

320

people. That was what it was meant to look like. And if the murderer had been content — only they never are — to leave well alone, it might have become an unsolved mystery. But the criminal feared that Nancy Royd knew something, so she had to go. That told me a lot. Here was a nice quiet case of poisoning, half-intended to look like suicide: an utterly different crime from the first. That meant I had to rearrange my ideas of the mental make-up of the criminal. It also told me that the first crime was not unpremeditated. It was a deliberate act of violence made to appear as if it was done on a blind impulse of fury.

'Next, Dr. Crawford was attacked by night in the wood and half-killed. It was obvious then that Dr. Crawford, too, knew something — consciously or unconsciously — that it was dangerous for her to know. The murderer should have killed her — er, I mean, from his point of view — that was a fatal error on his part. He made one other ludicrously simple slip, too, but I'll come back to that later.

'On the evidence of these crimes, I

proceeded to deduce certain points about the murderer. A brain that worked with great rapidity, for one thing, with a fairly high percentage of concentration. He would be characteristically brilliant and daringly impulsive. Yet his was a simple and uncomplex thought: once one found the right thread, it would be easy to follow. One might further presume that he was not very big or strong, since he was not able to overpower Dr. Crawford completely, although he had the advantage of taking her by surprise.' I stared round the room at them all, measuring them with my eyes.

'I had to admit,' I continued, 'that these were not characteristics of the hospital patients. On the contrary, the majority to a large extent showed marked lack of concentration; confused and intricate thought processes; timid and hesitating actions; and generally slow-moving brains. So I turned my attention to the psychology of the victims, particularly the first victim. How did his character agree or conflict with the criminal's? The first thing was that the late lamented was not very popular. His name might well have been Dr. Fell, for no one did like the poor chap, though nobody cared to say exactly why. As Dr. Ennis so neatly remarked on my first day here, there were plenty of reasons why he should have been killed, and plenty of people who might have done it — but that was my pigeon.' I smiled at Ennis encouragingly and he stared back blandly.

'Why did no one like Dr. Royd? I set myself to find an answer to that question. His patients vowed it was due to his methods of deep analysis that they so heartily disliked him; he didn't help them enough, made them suffer too much, and so on. His colleagues' opinions were severely divided on that point, some thinking he was a new and profounder Freud, others believing he was on the verge of megalomania. Then, from Mrs. Royd and others, I began to gather hints on his personality, and it did not seem to be a very pleasant one. Rather a tyrant; quietly domineering; fond of playing cat and mouse, it seemed; and — I summed up judgement in the word — amoral.

From hints dropped here and there by his wife and others, it was clear that he was sexually not inhibited. Then, bored with the administrative side, he so mismanaged the hospital that it was running at a considerable loss. Thereupon he proceeded to blackmail Dr. McIvor into paying back part of his salary to the hospital. Unfortunately for Royd, McIvor would not agree to this. He then utilised Dr. Chumly's admiration for him; offered, I expect, to speculate for him; and — er — *lost* the money. He may, of course, actually have speculated with the money, but I rather suspect that that money went straight into the hospital.' From the corner of my eye I could see Chumly was very pale. 'Yes, not at all a nice character, I'm afraid.

'Undoubtedly, Royd was a clever man, but with a one-track mind. Which side of his character had conflicted with his murderer's? Had it been a clash of two dominant personalities? Had it been a professional disagreement between colleagues? Or had it been a sort of religious disapproval of his amorality? Or fear of his power? Or — ? The possibilities were almost endless, and I followed them all up. One thing seemed odd in particular to me — that though it was suggested Royd was rather a womaniser, no evidence of this came to light. Now, *cherchez la femme* suits the national psychology of the French, but is not generally applicable here, by any means, we being a more frigid and less dramatic nation. Still, as I say, it did seem odd, and I began to hunt around for a woman in the case. The only suggestion of one I could find was Sister Hythe.' Dr. Ennis sniggered. 'Yes, it did seem almost laughable, and yet . . . I reserved judgement. When Mrs. Royd was killed, it appeared that the case was actually reversed: she had been the double-crosser. She had been having an affair with John Christie. She was going to have a baby, and she was genuinely terrified that her husband would find out. She might have killed him out of sheer terror, but she didn't. In fact, she thought her lover had. And he suspected her, but that is by the by.

'It was when I came across certain

extracts from Nancy Royd's diary that an idea suggested itself to me. Nancy Royd was afraid he would find out — and why? Not because he would do anything to her. She writes in one of her letters to Christie that he would watch and smile his peculiar kind of smile. Two or three times, she mentions in the letters and the diary that she thinks he is suspicious. Supposing now, I reasoned, that he *was* suspicious — not that Nancy was having an affair, but that she was pregnant. Was that a very unlikely thing for a husband and a doctor to suspect? We know that he wanted children, was disappointed at not having any, and we can imagine how elated he would be at discovering his prospective fatherhood. He was not the type to talk about it, at least at that early stage; he would keep it to himself. But, I argued, he would surely break off any old associations and devote himself, as he must have done in the early days of their married life, to his wife. In fact, I argued that he would turn over a new leaf — or try to. What do you think? Does that seem psychologically correct?'

Dr. McIvor said: 'Yes . . . I don't see why not . . . '

'Most improbable,' said Dr. Fortescue emphatically. 'He was not at all the type to change character in midstream. Much too self-satisfied and conceited. Once he made up his mind, nothing would move him.'

'Sorry, I agree with Dr. McIvor,' said Ennis. 'Fundamentally, like most bullies, he was a sentimentalist. Fatherhood was just the kind of emotional landmark to affect him deeply.'

I nodded. 'So much for that. And all these little jigsaw pieces muddled about in my brain. I had provisionally eliminated the patients. The staff were not so easy to eliminate. The elimination of Miss Brace meant that the first murder must have taken place between half-past nine and ten. From ten o'clock onward Miss Brace was on guard, so to speak, at one door; but anyway, if Royd had been alive after ten o'clock, he would have come out to fetch her as usual. Very well. From half-past nine to ten, you, Dr. McIvor, were seeing patients; and so were you, Dr.

Ennis; and you, Dr. Crawford. Dr. Chumly was in his cottage — alone. And Dr. Fortescue was in hers, although she was supposed to be hundreds of miles away. Anyone else? Oh, yes — Sister Hythe, who was nowhere in particular, but just generally 'about'. Yes, quite easy for her to have slipped in to Royd's for a few minutes, part of her duties to receive orders and so on; and even if she had been seen, no one would have thought anything of it. There was motive there, as well; more than a suggestion of an antique affair between her and Royd out in the backwoods of Australia. Maybe a little blackmail, too. Yet Hythe was hardly the type, I thought; she was not exactly clever, and she was so frankly spiteful and slanderous — more the type to murder reputations than lives, I should have said. Still, hell — if I may borrow a phrase — hath no fury like a woman scorned.

'On the other hand, I was definitely chary of accepting Dr. Fortescue's excuse for returning secretly to her house. The opportunity there stuck out a mile, except that if she was seen she was done for.

That meant taking a considerable risk — but the murderer did take the most formidable risks all the time. And, further, I bore in mind that the murderer made use of the scarcely known communicating door that led to the squash court. As for motive . . . ' I looked across at her, sitting there as calm and pale as an ivory idol. 'You didn't approve of him at all, did you, Doctor? You believed that he overstepped the mark with his patients sometimes, and did not always use his power over them for their good. He was too self-important and not sufficiently humble. Besides, you loved little Nancy Royd, didn't you? You must have been very distressed when she told you those intimate details about some of Royd's nasty little ways. Mmm!

'Then there was Dr. Chumly. What an opportunity he had. If he was noticed roaming about the hospital, it wouldn't really matter; any fudged-up excuse would do. And as for motive . . . He may have discovered that Royd was calmly appropriating the money he had guilelessly entrusted to him for speculation. Or it might indeed be a case of *cherchez la femme* . . . What do you say, Chumly?'

Chumly rose, stuttering with fury. 'You may think you're bloody funny . . . standing there t-trying t-to make me look a fool . . . But I think it's d-damned bad form . . . and I don't mean to stay here to be insulted . . . '

I said, 'Oh, come, Dr. Chumly, you must try not to rise so easily to the bait. Ask Dr. McIvor, he's a fisherman: he'll tell you what a dangerous thing it is to do. I'm only telling you a story, you know; surely you won't leave before I have finished.' He returned sulkily to his seat, and I resumed.

'When you've got *how* you've got *who*. That's a detective maxim. But I was very far from knowing *how*. I had a pretty good idea after the inquest *how* Nancy Royd was killed. At the post-mortem, the stomach was found to be practically empty, and faint traces of mercury were found among the viscera. It did not require a great brain to deduce that she had taken a strong purgative. But when and why? Had she taken it, or had the

330

murderer induced her to take it? I puzzled about this till I learnt that calomel leaves strongish trails of mercury behind it. Then I understood. She didn't take it herself; the murderer gave it to her so that at some later date convenient to the *murderer* she would be attacked by sudden cramping pains, inexplicable and rather alarming. She would almost certainly ask for help, and — there the way lay open for the murderer to supply the apparently harmless capsules that in reality contained a deadly amount of morphia.' Someone drew in a breath sharply. I paused and surveyed them.

'Mmm! We know that Dr. Fortescue supplied the morphia from her private stock,' I went on, 'large quantities of which she had acquired on her visit to London. She probably already had some, too. Did anyone else know of these private supplies? And had they access to them? That is important. Be that as it may, however, I understand that Dr. Fortescue has a weakness for patent medicines — a kind of hobby, I gather. She'll find some new cure-all and stick to it for months, offering it freely to her friends and dosing her patients with it on every possible occasion.' Dr. Fortescue avoided my eye. 'No harm in it, I suppose, even if there is no particular good; but on this occasion she was interested in some powdered nonsense put up in capsule form. Easy to tip out the contents and refill the little gelatine containers with a precisely calculated amount of morphia. The murderer knew that at a more or less certain time Nancy Royd would get in touch with Dr. Fortescue and complain of not feeling well, complain of pain, and then all the doctor had to do was to give or send her the phial of capsules. As easy as pie. And that is just what did happen. Of course, we must remember that the morphia may have been inserted after the capsules had left Dr. Fortescue's hands, and before they were put into Nancy's.' Chumly munched his fingers in angry silence. 'Anyhow, Dr. Chumly, with his psychological technique, prevailed on her to take the capsules. It was unfortunate for the murderer that Nancy Royd had already written a letter to her lover denouncing who she suspected as the murderer. In fact, she was murdered for nothing.' Mary winced and pressed the back of her hand across her eyes as if they hurt her.

'Yes, that was all simple enough. But what happened next? Dr. Crawford was attacked. She was inveigled by night into the wood, and there someone leapt on her from a tree and tried to strangle her with her scarf. Dr. Crawford was not sure whether it was a man or a woman, but she *thought* it was a man. But, as I said before, it could not be a very tall man, or a very strong man.' I could see the three male doctors shrinking beneath my penetrating stare till they felt no larger than Gulliver among the Brobdingnagians.

'That a crime did not actually occur was no thanks to me. It was the second time I had fallen down on the job. But Dr. Crawford nobly bore me no malice, repeated the story to me and helped me to reconstruct the scene. Then this one enormously important tiny mistake emerged and stared me in the face. Impossible to ignore its significance. All the maddening jigsaw pieces lying about my brain suddenly slid into place . . . and, unmistakably, fitted one person. I knew that if my deductions were right, they must fit one person, and one person only. I almost wished I was wrong, but there it was — inescapably. Only I still did not know how. How could I break down that Monday morning alibi? That was what worried me. Until I could prove the first crime, I could not prove the second. However, this morning Mrs. Harrison was chatting to me down at The Three Crows, and she let drop a remark quite casually that made the whole thing as lucid as sunlight. Immediately I raced up here to verify it. I was right: it was so; and it was as I came triumphantly away that I heard that Christie had been killed. I had been just too late again, and failed to save his life. But I know how he was killed.'

I turned to Helen. 'He had an appointment with you today, didn't he?'

'Yes,' she said, quietly.

'Did he keep it?'

She shook her head.

'And you, of course, thought nothing of it. Why should you? But Christie had received Nancy's letter from Chumly then. What happened then, I cannot be quite sure. Did he mean to tell me? Did the murderer chance to come upon him at that moment, and perhaps see the letter? Or did he go rashly and accuse the murderer to his face? However it may have been, he must have been with the murderer, and he did not mean to let him go away again. So he proceeded to hypnotise him. I want you to bear in mind that the murderer is a doctor — to put it plainly, is one of yourselves,' I said solemnly, staring at their bent heads, all studiously avoiding one another's eyes. 'It was easy for him. He knew exactly how to go about the business of hypnotising a person to make them do what you want them to do — '

'Tchah!' exclaimed Dr. McIvor impatiently. 'Are you trying to tell us that a person can be hypnotised into committing suicide? Do you realise, my good man, that you cannot hypnotise a person into doing a thing against his will?'

'He might have had suicidal tendencies,' murmured Ennis.

'It doesn't matter really,' I said blandly. 'Though I am only a layman, I can see many ways of inducing a person to obey one quite readily. For example, it might be suggested that he write a letter saying so-and-so (nothing very conflict-causing there), then it would be suggested that he will feel hot or stifling, and he will wander round till he comes to a certain staircase — or whatever it is that leads to the tricksy battlements — from which he will find his way to the roof. Once up among the ramparts, he will be overcome by the height, perhaps, as he looks over the edge; or stumble, fall, and not be able to recover himself. Oh, it would be a terribly easy thing to do with a hypnotic subject — as Christie was.'

'Possible, possible,' mumbled McIvor.

'It was the clue of hypnosis that Mrs. Harrison gave me,' I continued. 'The problem had been, you see, how a doctor could leave his patient for even five minutes without endangering himself. He might make an excuse to leave his patient for a few minutes, but if there were tiresome enquiries later, the patient would be sure to remember an awkward, undesirable fact like that. Besides, even the most cold-blooded murderer would surely be a trifle disturbed, flustered or out of breath. But the possibility of hypnosis altered all that. Let me try a little mental reconstruction. Visualise, about half-past nine on that Monday morning, a doctor staring abstractedly out of his window and thinking his own dark murderous thoughts, while a patient determinedly chatters symptoms the other side of the room. Before his unseeing gaze, Gresly slinks off to the woods to keep his appointment with the blackmailing boy when he should have been keeping his appointment with Royd. Suddenly, he realises that unconsciously-assimilated fact consciously, realises that it means that Royd is alone . . . But *he* is not alone, *he* has a patient . . . What an opportunity . . . If only, somehow . . . Perhaps the thought comes to him then that the patient provides an excellent alibi. You know, I stipulated a quick brain, active and daring. Probably the basic details of the simple but bold plot spring into his mind while he is submerging Miss Wylie — for she was the patient in question — in a deep hypnotic sleep. The doctor is then free to ... to run downstairs, through the communicating door, pick up the poker and smash it down on Dr. Royd's unprotected skull — '

A little moan interrupted me, and Mary Fortescue slumped sideways off her chair.

We bent over her.

'Not — not Mary?' said McIvor in a half-stifled, incredulous whisper.

'Why should it be?' said Ennis through his teeth.

'Miss Wylie was her patient.'

'But Dr. Fortescue was away on holiday,' I reminded them, and watched them draw away and stand looking at one another with ill-concealed nervousness. 'One of you had taken over Miss Wylie.'

Dr. Fortescue struggled into an upright position. 'Please forgive me for being so foolish ... the strain ... run-down, and nerves not too good ... '

Helen stood in front of me, still and pale. 'I took over Miss Wylie while Mary was away. Are you accusing me?'

I looked down at her thoughtfully. 'Yes.'

'Me?' Her voice was an indignant squeak. If this was not innocence, it was well-simulated. 'I've never heard of such a fantastic rigmarole in my life. You must be mad! A lot of rot about hypnosis, and far-fetched hypotheses about motives and characteristics and more nonsense of the same sort, and not one solitary honest-to-God proof to bless yourself with. Try something a little less half-baked next time, Mr. Chaos,' she said with a short laugh. 'Why should *I* kill Dr. Royd? I didn't even dislike the poor man . . . '

'Of course, you didn't kill him because you disliked him. On the contrary. It was because you loved him.'

She grinned at me. 'Jealous, Jacob?'

'Not my temperament. But yours, yes. You had had an affair with him, and then he threw you over, wasn't that it?'

'Threw *me* over, damn your eyes! Impudent swine!' Eyes blazing, she hit me with all her strength across the face. I caught her hand and pinioned it to her side. She began to scream shrilly; berating me for my villainy, berating the doctors for not coming to her assistance against me. She kicked. She bit. And the doctors stood in a frigid, shocked little group about McIvor's desk and watched me hold her at bay. I had to admit that even in her temper she was lovely; no, even lovelier now she had let go her reserve and showed the fire and sparkle that was hidden at other times. I yanked her other arm behind her roughly. In the struggle, her spectacles fell off and smashed into fragments on the ground. She glared at me from her lovely, misty-grey, myopic eyes.

I said: 'Don't you remember? That was the silly but oh-so-important mistake you made before, when you were attacked — or, at least, when you attacked yourself in the wood. You forgot to smash or lose your glasses during your struggles. You turned up after your nasty ordeal, torn, bleeding and shaken — but without so much as a scratch on your glasses. And yet, when you reconstructed the scene with me, you were careful to remove them and place them on the mantelpiece for fear they should be injured in the struggle.'

My arms encircled her, holding her wrists down behind her back. She stood quietly within my clasp. I could feel her heart banging against her side.

'Yes,' she said. 'I remember. By God, what a damn silly mistake. You would think my neck was worth a pair of glasses, wouldn't you? But, you know, when one always wears them they seem to become a part of one, like an extra limb. I didn't give them a thought. Besides, it was no joke, believe me, sitting in that hateful dark wood, trying to strangle oneself . . . There's something about woods . . . I began to get absolutely panic-stricken . . . It seemed to be full of . . . and then I had an idea that Maurice and Nancy . . . I started running and bumping into trees . . . I thought someone was after me . . . I fell . . . tore my skirt on a tree . . . I was almost at screaming point when I found you . . . No mistake about that . . . And I forgot my glasses . . . I lost my head in

341

there — and so, I suppose, I shall lose it again,' she said with wry humour. 'At the time, it seemed a good idea.'

'Yes, it might have worked. It does sometimes,' I said wearily. I felt as tired as if I had run a four-mile dash. I let her go.

'I told you that Harrison bitch always makes trouble, didn't I? If she'd only kept her bloody trap shut . . . ' She shrugged.

Mary, somewhat recovered, came toward us. Her arm shook slightly as she put it with a tender gesture about Helen's shoulders.

'I don't believe a word of it. It's nonsense, Helen. I know you didn't do it. Don't say a word until you have seen a lawyer, otherwise anything you say may be used in evidence against you, you know. It's some ridiculous mistake and we'll soon put it right.'

With a superbly dignified gesture, Helen drew away.

'Don't be more of a fool than you can help, Mary. What is the use of pretending now? There's a time for everything, as your pet Ecclesiastes said. Of course, I did it; and he knows I did,' she affirmed, pointing to me.

'You mean, you killed Maurice?' she asked incredulously.

Helen nodded.

'And little Nancy . . . ? And Christie . . . ?'

'I suppose so. It never seemed very real to me — not being there at the time; not actually doing it. I never meant to kill *them*; it was unavoidable. Maurice was different, the swine!' She turned to me. 'You were surprisingly right. I don't know how you know . . . Maurice and I had been lovers for over a year. I'd been in love before, but it was the first time I had loved like that. I adored him. I wasn't apart from him at all; he was my perfect complement. And I thought he felt for me what I felt for him. He always gave me to understand that his wife didn't mean a thing to him. She was cold, he said.' She gave a wry, contemptuous laugh. 'I learnt my error on that score when he came to see me for the last time . . . When was it . . . ? Saturday week. Oh, God, is it less than a fortnight ago?' The colour fled from her cheeks, and she veiled the sudden anguish in her eyes.

'He came to dinner that Saturday as usual — it was a custom with us — but I noticed the difference in him at once. He was preoccupied, didn't eat, fidgeted, and there was an undefinable something . . . At last, it came out. Nancy was going to have a baby. I wouldn't believe it at first. I thought it was a ruse to get him back — 'trying it on', as women so often do. He swore that she had not even mentioned it to him: too shy, probably, or uncertain. But he knew.

'I said: 'But you always told me that there was nothing between you and Nancy, since we . . . '

' 'Did I?' he said indifferently. 'What does it matter now what I said? That's all done with.'

' 'Do you mean . . . ?'

' 'I'm trying to tell you, Helen, if you'll listen. This is the end. We've had a perfectly grand time, and I shall always have most pleasant and grateful memories . . . Now it's over.'

' 'Over?' I echoed, stupidly. 'You can't finish a love affair just like that. You must have a reason.' I was just talking for time, you see.

'He sneered down at me. 'Oh, reasons! I'll give you a dozen, if that's what you want. I'll say it's because of Nan. Or the child. Or because people are getting suspicious. Or just because I'm sick to death of you. Take any reason you like, I don't mind. So long as you understand that it really is over, and don't start making scenes or trying to win me back, I don't care what you think.'

'I don't know what I said . . . I lost control . . . It didn't matter, though. In the middle of my raging, he took up his hat and walked out.' She closed her eyes. 'Sunday was a day of absolute torment. I thought I would go crazy. I simply could not believe that it was all over, that anyone could do that to me . . . When I thought of Maurice's face when he said he was sick of me . . . ' She shuddered. 'It seemed as though Monday would never come.

'Monday did come, and when we met for the daily conference I noticed, with a pang of misery, how he avoided my eye. I saw to it that I was the last to leave the room . . . actually, I slipped back. I shut the door behind me and stood facing him. He looked up irritably from his writing and asked me what I wanted. Funnily enough, my carefully-thought-out speech had vanished. My mind was a blank.

'He stood up impatiently. 'Don't let us have any more scenes, please, Helen. This is neither the time nor the place for that sort of thing.'

' 'You're very sure of yourself, aren't you, Maurice?' I said. 'What do you suppose Nancy would feel about it if she knew?'

' 'About our affair, do you mean?' He laughed. 'Good Lord, I've never hidden anything like that from her, my dear girl. It wasn't important enough to give a second thought to.'

'I went away then . . . to my consulting room . . . and presently Miss Wylie came along. It was as you said: I leant against the window, pretending to listen to Miss Wylie, and really trying to comprehend that for me the light of life was quenched.

I could hear his damned cruel voice saying again and again that he was sick of me, and his bored blank eyes turning contemptuously from mine . . . I couldn't bear it . . . I felt I would burst beneath the tremendous burden of fury and sick resentment that I bore . . . I wanted to strangle him . . . or smash him . . . or . . . It was only by hurting him as he had hurt me that I could find balm for myself, I knew . . . The whole weekend, I'd been trying to think of a way to pay him back . . .

'Subconsciously, I must have seen Gresly going toward the spinney, and then its significance struck me. I realised he was alone. I could go and see him again . . . Bit by bit it dawned on me that I had a perfect opportunity — complete with alibi and all — to . . . kill him.

'With Miss Wylie asleep, I drew a surgical rubber glove onto my right hand, jammed it in my pocket, and ran downstairs. I utilised it to open the connecting door without leaving finger-prints. He didn't hear me when I came in. He was still sitting at the desk writing.

There was something touchingly boyish, ingenuous about the back of his head. I could have wept. I thought wildly that I must have made a mistake, it just couldn't be true. I put my right hand back in my pocket, and said: 'You didn't really mean you were sick of me, did you, Maurice?'

'He swung half-round in his chair then, and his face was absolutely savage with fury as he shouted at me: 'My God, yes, yes, yes! How many more times do I need to tell you that you bore me to tears? I could scream at the sight of you; you bore me so. Is that plain enough? For God's sake, do leave me alone. You're an absolute vampire.'

'That was that. I turned on my heel as if to go. I shut the connecting door. Quietly, I picked up the poker. Once more he was bent over his desk, oblivious . . . I stood behind him, and brought the poker-butt down on his head . . . It was like crushing an eggshell with a teaspoon. I was surprised to find how easy it was . . . It was nothing at all . . . It was funny to think that just two or three blows with

348

a lump of brass could annihilate a man . . . Maurice was gone, and all that remained was a mass of meaningless matter . . .

'Then I did feel a little queer. I had to get away quickly. I dropped the blood-stained poker by his side and hurried away, locking the door behind me. I think my idea there must have been vaguely to postpone discovery for a little while; at least, until I was recovered and had dealt with Miss Wylie.'

She gave a little shiver. 'Everything was as smooth as butter till you came along,' she said reproachfully. 'Not a twinge of conscience or regret. Not a doubt or suspicion from anyone. The police questioning was the sheerest formality. Then you came along and asked stuffy questions about missing keys and suchlike, and — as you realised — I felt it safer to be friends with you and help you all I could. The joke was that I often found myself helping you against my own interests.' She laughed.

'But what about little Nancy?' asked Dr. Fortescue, in a colourless voice. 'Why did you kill her?'

Dr. Crawford stared at her in silence. At last: 'That dreadful Sunday . . . ' she mused. 'She came to me and said she must speak to me. She sat there with her pretty, silly little face, and slayed me with one sentence.

' 'You killed Maurice for nothing, you know. The child wasn't his at all.' That was what she said, with her chocolate-box smile. 'You see, you really needn't have killed him, after all.' On and on she babbled. How I didn't kill her there and then, I don't know. I suppose I was too dazed. 'Of course,' she said, 'Maurice would want to break with you because of it; he was really a very honourable man, and madly in love with me.' On and on . . .

'I said: 'Why are you telling me this? If you think I killed your husband, why don't you tell the police?'

'That was her business, she said. How did I know that that was not just what she was going to do?

' 'You mean, you haven't any proof,' I said.

'At this point, the porter rang through to say you wanted to see me, Chaos. Dared I . . . ? I decided to risk it, on the assumption that my wits were quicker than hers. I think now that she was giving me a warning to commit suicide if I was guilty. Jolly decent of her, really. She was quite a nice kid, and I wish . . . However, I told the porter to send you up.

'Meanwhile, I was frantically planning, my thoughts flying all over the place . . . What could I do . . . ? Then the first step into a misty vista of escape presented itself, while you were talking away to us. Nancy said she took saccharine in her tea, remember? The tiny white tablet I dropped in was not saccharine, but calomel . . . You know the rest.

'When she had gone, I felt — terrible. The strain had been terrific; no wonder you noticed I looked queer. And then, like a sword ripping me up, it struck me that I had killed Maurice needlessly. That, in fact, everything had been in my favour if only I had been more patient about it . . . for, once he discovered that the child was someone else's . . . It wasn't till that terrible moment that the full realisation of Maurice's death came home to me. Even though I had killed him with my own hands, it hadn't seemed real to me till then . . . He was gone, and it was *my* fault . . . I felt as though I would die with grief. If only I had been alone just then . . . but you were there, and I had to try and control my agony. It was the bitterest moment I have ever known . . . I wanted to cry and wail aloud . . . ' She rocked to and fro as she described her sufferings retrospectively.

'I fudged up all that rot about Mary for you afterwards, but it sounded very thin to my ears, and I never really felt quite safe with you again from that moment.

'You remember, Mary, how I came round to see you? It was so easy to get you out of the way . . . You picked me some of those lovely zinnias, dear, you remember? So sweet of you . . . And while you picked them, I got rid of the rubbish in the capsules and filled them up with morphia from Mary's supply. Replaced the phial of capsules in the cupboard and strolled out to join you in the garden,

Mary, and invite you to dinner. I wanted to have you under my eye — just in case. Chumly and Chaos, too; and the stage was set for the second act.'

She sat in gloomy silence for a while. 'What a dreadful day that Sunday was. I was completely disorientated from shock and misery. And then Miss Brace . . . I behaved awfully stupidly there. Brace had all the cards stacked against her, and I could easily have persuaded you she was the murderess. Instead of that, either professional instinct or pity for that poor little rat — or God knows what — made me lose my head. I showed you that she could not have done it. In my opinion,' she added dispassionately, 'that was when I lost the game. Ah, but I had bad luck! How was I to know that she would leave a letter behind? And Chumly so nearly forgot it. Then Christie scared the blue daylights out of me that time. It was so utterly unforeseen. The only thing I could think of then was to stage that attack on myself. But I think in my heart of hearts I knew by this time that I was playing a losing game. I don't think I'm really cut out to be a murderess. And the luck hadn't been with me. I never wanted to kill Maurice: I loved him . . . But he was so dreadful to me. And it was nothing but sheer bad luck that made me kill poor little Nancy. Christie, too . . . Killing Maurice was like a horrible accident, and everything that happened after that followed on naturally as a consequence of that ghastly mistake. You can see that, can't you?' she pleaded. 'When it was Nancy's life or mine, looked at logically, I was a far more useful and important person. There was no other way I could reasonably act.'

'What happened with Christie?'

'He must have got that letter just before the interview. He came in to me, the fool, and accused me to my face. Showed me the letter when I wouldn't believe it. I just laughed at it and denied that there was a word of truth in it. But he stormed up and down until he brought on one of his attacks. I quieted him down and hypnotised him, as I always did when he had an attack. I thought out the position, and there seemed only one thing to do. It was pretty much as you suggested, Jacob. My God, you are a clever chap; you don't look as smart as that, you know.'

'You know my methods, Watson. The little grey cells and all that. It's all this modern farrago called psychology. But I had no heart for it.'

'When did you begin to suspect?'

'Suspect! We always suspect everyone, you know that. It was very convenient having you under my eye all the time.' She looked depressed, and I added, 'Very easy on the eye you were, too.'

She smiled. 'What a nice man you are. I was getting really fond of you. You know, I was seriously thinking of marrying you — a husband can't give evidence against his wife, can he? That's what I should have done. Too late now . . . What happens next?'

'That's the end, I'm afraid.'

'Surely not,' she said calmly. 'Surely you gentlemen are not going to allow a public scandal to occur. It would absolutely mean the end of the hospital if it comes out that one of the doctors went in for murder in quite a big way . . . Imagine the sensation the trial would cause; and then, if I was convicted, my — my execution . . . ' Her assurance was superb.

His gaze directed on his clasped hands, Dr. McIvor said quietly: 'I don't think it will come to that, Dr. Crawford. I think whatever trial there is will be very quiet and quick, and then it will be . . . Broadmoor . . . for life . . . '

'Broadmoor?' And as it sank home, I saw her crumple and wilt as if some inner dominant force had collapsed and there was no longer any way to hold the shell of her personality together. 'Am *I* insane . . . ?' she asked in a whisper of wondering horror from somewhere a long way away.

I opened the door and Trevor, who had been patiently awaiting his cue, came in.

I heard the bracelets snap to. The three of us walked silently from the room. In the corridor, I turned to Trevor.

'Have you found out how to get her away without being seen?'

He nodded. 'The back way, the way

they take out the dead 'uns, down the corpse-chute. You don't come with us, do you? No. Well, so long, maestro,' he said cheerily. 'Next time I come, I'll bring my autograph album.' They moved away.

I leant up against the window and watched them go. I could not face the others just then. It had been a hateful case, and I was glad it was over.

Far below me Helen climbed into the police-car. Her hair gleamed brightly in the cold, autumnal sunlight. I tried not to think. I put the unpleasant but gifted doctor, his pretty wife and her handsome lover in the scales against Helen. I tried to believe they would lie more quietly now they were avenged. I tried to feel that it was the end of just another case.

But all the time, I was seeing with her eyes the fiery trees waving their flame-clad branches to and fro in the same small, sharp wind that smartingly caressed my face; the curved flight of a bird as it breasted a current of air; and hearing shouted laughter carried on the breeze; glimpsing through her drowning eyes visions of the fine, free world she would never see again.

The car shot suddenly away, taking her from me forever.

We do hope that you have enjoyed reading this large print book.

Did you know that all of our titles are available for purchase?

We publish a wide range of high quality large print books including:

**Romances, Mysteries, Classics**
**General Fiction**
**Non Fiction and Westerns**

Special interest titles available in large print are:

**The Little Oxford Dictionary**
**Music Book, Song Book**
**Hymn Book, Service Book**

Also available from us courtesy of Oxford University Press:

**Young Readers' Dictionary**
**(large print edition)**
**Young Readers' Thesaurus**
**(large print edition)**

For further information or a free brochure, please contact us at:
**Ulverscroft Large Print Books Ltd.,**
**The Green, Bradgate Road, Anstey,**
**Leicester, LE7 7FU, England.**
**Tel:** (00 44) **0116 236 4325**
**Fax:** (00 44) **0116 234 0205**

*Other titles in the*
*Linford Mystery Library:*

# THIS IS THE HOUSE

## Shelley Smith

On a picturesque West Indies island, the capital is dominated by the house on the mountaintop: the house that Jacques built. Premier Justice Antoine Jacques was divinely happy with his beautiful wife Julia and their son Raoul — until Julia was stricken with total paralysis . . . For years now, La Morte, as she is known, has been confined to her bed. Then, one day, she is found dead. And Quentin Seal, author of detective stories, is begged by Antoine to investigate . . .

# THE SNARK WAS A BOOJUM

## Gerald Verner

When William Baker is found dead, his naked and twisted body lying under a bench in the dingy waiting room of a train station, the village police are baffled. Soon afterward another corpse appears, this time posthumously stuffed into full evening dress, with black pigment smeared on his face. A murderer is at large whose M.O. is to use his victims to recreate scenes from Lewis Carroll's nonsense poem, 'The Hunting of the Snark' — and it's up to amateur detective Simon Gale to stop him before he kills again.

# JUNGLE QUEST

## Denis Hughes

For several months, the British and European security agencies in Africa have been intercepting coded secret radio messages that are being received and responded to by a radio station hidden in the almost impenetrable depths of the Congo jungle. It's clear that some dastardly international plot is afoot. A top agent is despatched to investigate, but his reports cease abruptly, and weeks pass without further communication from him. So renowned jungle explorer Rex Brandon is hired to head an expedition to locate and neutralise the danger . . .